BLUE OCTAVO

JOHN BLACKBURN was born in 1923 in the village of Corbridge, England, the second son of a clergyman. Blackburn started attending Haileybury College near London in 1937, but his education was interrupted by the onset of World War II; the shadow of the war, and that of Nazi Germany, would later play a role in many of his works. He served as a radio officer during the war in the Mercantile Marine from 1942 to 1945, and resumed his education afterwards at Durham University, earning his bachelor's degree in 1949. Blackburn taught for several years after that, first in London and then in Berlin, and married Joan Mary Clift in 1950. Returning to London in 1952, he took over the management of Red Lion Books.

It was there that Blackburn began writing, and the immediate success in 1958 of his first novel, *A Scent of New-Mown Hay*, led him to take up a career as a writer full time. He and his wife also maintained an antiquarian bookstore, a secondary career that would inform some of Blackburn's work, including *Blue Octavo* (1963). *A Scent of New-Mown Hay* typified the approach that would come to characterize Blackburn's twenty-eight novels, which defied easy categorization in their unique and compelling mixture of the genres of science fiction, horror, mystery, and thriller. Many of Blackburn's best novels came in the late 1960s and early 1970s, with a string of successes that included the classics *A Ring of Roses* (1965), *Children of the Night* (1966), *Nothing but the Night* (1968; adapted for a 1973 film starring Christopher Lee and Peter Cushing), *Devil Daddy* (1972) and *Our Lady of Pain* (1974). Somewhat unusually for a popular horror writer, Blackburn's novels were not only successful with the reading public but also won widespread critical acclaim: the *Times Literary Supplement* declared him 'today's master of horror' and compared him with the Grimm Brothers, while the *Penguin Encyclopedia of Horror and the Supernatural* regarded him as 'certainly the best British novelist in his field' and the *St. James Guide to Crime & Mystery Writers* called him 'one of England's best practicing novelists in the tradition of the thriller novel'.

By the time Blackburn published his final novel in 1985, much of his work was already out of print, an inexplicable neglect that largely continued until Valancourt began republishing his novels in 2013. John Blackburn died in 1993.

MIKE RIPLEY is an award-winning British author, a respected critic of crime fiction and the series editor of the *Top Notch Thrillers* imprint, which has proudly reissued John Blackburn's 1968 novel *The Young Man from Lima*.

By John Blackburn

A Scent of New-Mown Hay (1958)★

A Sour Apple Tree (1958)

Broken Boy (1959)★

Dead Man Running (1960)

The Gaunt Woman (1962)

Blue Octavo (1963)★

Colonel Bogus (1964)

The Winds of Midnight (1964)

A Ring of Roses (1965)

Children of the Night (1966)

The Flame and the Wind (1967)★

Nothing but the Night (1968)★

The Young Man from Lima (1968)

Bury Him Darkly (1969)★

Blow the House Down (1970)

The Household Traitors (1971)★

Devil Daddy (1972)

For Fear of Little Men (1972)

Deep Among the Dead Men (1973)

Our Lady of Pain (1974)★

Mister Brown's Bodies (1975)

The Face of the Lion (1976)★

The Cyclops Goblet (1977)★

Dead Man's Handle (1978)

The Sins of the Father (1979)

A Beastly Business (1982)★

The Book of the Dead (1984)

The Bad Penny (1985)★

★ Available or forthcoming from Valancourt Books

JOHN BLACKBURN

Blue Octavo

With a new introduction by
MIKE RIPLEY

VALANCOURT BOOKS
Richmond, Virginia
2013

Blue Octavo by John Blackburn
First published London: Jonathan Cape, 1963
Original U.S. title: *Bound to Kill*
First Valancourt Books edition 2013

Published by Valancourt Books, Richmond, Virginia
Publisher & Editor: JAMES D. JENKINS
20th Century Series Editor: SIMON STERN, University of Toronto
http://www.valancourtbooks.com

ISBN 978-1-939140-73-9

Cover art by M. S. Corley
Set in Dante MT 11/14

INTRODUCTION

IN his native Britain, John Fenwick Blackburn (1923-1993) and his books are disgracefully forgotten, perhaps because his fiction rarely fell into a single, convenient category. He wrote thrillers – that much booksellers and critics could usually agree on – and they were fast-paced, suspenseful, action-packed thrillers too, often encompassing the Cold War spy story and forecasting the threat of biological weapons of mass destruction. Yet what distinguished Blackburn from contemporaries such as Alistair MacLean, Desmond Bagley, Gavin Lyall and Len Deighton, was that he spiced his fiction with a sprinkling of science fiction, a touch of the supernatural, a goodly dash of Gothic horror and a large portion of the macabre.

In fact Blackburn was the literary bridge in popular horror fiction between the work of Dennis Wheatley and James Herbert, and for that alone he deserves to be remembered. Ironically, the novel he is best remembered for in the UK, at least by booksellers and bibliophiles, is his 1963 thriller *Blue Octavo* (published in America as *Bound To Kill*), which is probably the most conventional mystery he ever published, containing no supernatural or science-fiction elements and a limited amount of the macabre. (Only one priest is tortured before being burned to death, which by Blackburn's standards is quite restrained!)

The reason for *Blue Octavo*'s popularity among booksellers and bibliophiles is because it is set in the world of antique and rare book-dealing, a shady world if ever there was one, as was also shown in George Sims's 1964 thriller *The Terrible Door*. Both John Blackburn and George Sims were themselves rare book dealers and knew the world they described, and those two novels are often spoken of in the same breath when English booksellers of a certain age start to reminisce over their port and cigars.

The 'blue octavo' of the title is *The Grey Boulders*, an obscure, limited edition book on British rock climbing published in 1910. Only 100 copies were printed and almost half of them were destroyed in a warehouse fire; consequently, by 1963 copies are thin on the ground but even so, those that do appear for sale seem to command suspiciously high prices. Blackburn lays this out for the reader in an opening chapter describing the 'ringing' of a rare book auction, where dealers conspire in a 'ring' to keep bids artificially low, then conduct a second, private auction among themselves; and introduces one of his heroes, the young, slightly innocent and fairly honest bookseller John Cain.

When an older and far shadier bookseller who has paid well over the odds for a 'ring' copy of *Grey Boulders* is found hanged in his shop, an apparent suicide, Cain discovers the book is missing and that the dead dealer has, in recent months, bought up 30 copies, though why and for whom remains a mystery. Tracking down the few remaining copies becomes the 'McGuffin' of the plot of the novel until a copy is finally found and appears to be nothing more than a rather boring illustrated book about British mountaineering and climbers in the years 1840-1910, including the brothers Hal and William Lent, whose descendants now control the multi-million pound family business empire.

To unravel the mystery inside the blue octavo Cain needs the help of the bombastic egotist Moldon Mott – a self-publicist, author, explorer and, conveniently, rock climber. (Rock climbing was a hobby of Blackburn's.) It is the outrageous Mott who actually stumbles (almost literally) on the secret contained in *Grey Boulders* and who gives Blackburn the chance to slip in some sly observations such as: 'Two people had died probably because of a book called *Grey Boulders* and Mr Mott hadn't enjoyed himself so much for years.' There is also a very funny scene where the odious Mott (who complains that the British Museum is full of 'blackamoors and Indian students these days') is courted by a publisher under the misguided impression that Mott wants to change publishing houses.

John Cain and Moldon Mott are a formidable double-act, who stumble and bluff their way to the bottom of the mystery, but it is of course the handsome young bookseller who faces the murderer (in a climactic scene recalling the temptation of Christ by the Devil) and wins the beautiful girl in the end. And it is at the very end that Blackburn allows himself a flash of his trade-mark use of the macabre: 'It took him perhaps ten seconds to reach the ground, and pieces were torn from his body as he fell.'

Blue Octavo appeared in 1963 and was Blackburn's sixth novel, following several thrillers containing supernatural elements, evil scientists, ex-Nazis and spies, and after *Blue Octavo* he published a book a year up to 1979, most of them with a strong horror content, which resulted in the *Times Literary Supplement* awarding him the title 'today's master of horror'.

Most of Blackburn's novels were short – *Blue Octavo* clocks in at little more than 50,000 words, which is a refreshing change from many of today's overblown thrillers – and all characterised by short scenes, pithy dialogue and rapid action to enhance the pace of the storytelling. The characters in them are described in stark outlines, yet cleverly enough to make them all believable and though *Blue Octavo* may have only 50,000 words, you would be hard pressed to find a wasted one.

Blue Octavo may not be representative of Blackburn's main *oeuvre*, but it is a fine crime novel which stands the test of time well and its reissue should be a cause for rejoicing. At the time of writing this introduction, I could find only a single (ex-library) copy for sale in the UK, but I am sure that somewhere the ghost of John Blackburn the bookseller is quietly working out how much a first edition hardback (bound in blue boards of course) would be worth now, and possibly speculating on what lengths someone might go to get their hands on one . . .

MIKE RIPLEY

September 1, 2013

BLUE OCTAVO

One

'AND that, ladies and gentlemen, as the Duke said to the Duchess, appears to conclude our business for the day.'

Officially the sale was over. The auctioneer had cracked his last joke and climbed down from the pulpit-like desk, the public were drifting away, and the porters had started to shift the lots. The 'boys' grinned at each other and moved furtively to the door. The real auction was about to begin.

They slunk down the drive like wolves fearing ambush, not in a group which might hint of conspiracy, but in loping twos and threes, bowler or trilby hat pulled low over pallid, crafty faces, nicotine-stained fingers clutching catalogues, and thin, city shoes squelching on the muddy path; the furniture dealers to a van by the gate, and booksellers into the damp wood. Twelve men standing among the trees and bidding for lots they had already bought. The Ring going into action.

It was a lovely day: winter breaking into spring, with buds coming out on the trees, and a few crocuses still showing. They weren't interested in spring, or buds, or crocuses. They were just interested in their well-marked catalogues. Twenty lots had been sold to one of their members for a song, while the others had stood and kept quiet; for why should dog eat dog? Now the official owner would put those lots up for sale again, and the knock-out would show their true value.

'Well, gentlemen, I think we may as well begin.' With the air of a clergyman opening a sale of work, Jack Goldsmith leaned back against a tree and raised his white, fleshy hand.

'Yes, let me see. Lot Ninety-Three was the first, and it was sold to us for eight pounds. What may I start at, please? Thank you, Mr Callaghan – fifteen then. Mr Burton – eighteen. Mr Cain – twenty. Mr Callaghan – twenty-one. Sold to you, Bill, for twenty-one pounds; leaving us with thirteen to be divided as a dividend.

'Now, let's take Ninety-Four: the collection of sporting prints which, owing to the intervention of that very tiresome and persistent woman, reached twelve ten. Thank you, Mr Algar, we'll begin at eighteen then – '

Slowly and quietly, without excitement or rancour, the business was transacted; books for the highest bidder, and a share in the kitty for those who lost or merely kept quiet. A nice little kitty, too. Often the difference between what a lot had fetched at the sale and what it reached in the knock-out was as much as three hundred per cent. All very friendly and respectable. They were almost at the end of the catalogue when a note of tenseness crept into the proceedings.

'Twenty pounds, gentlemen.' Roach stood a little apart from the rest of the 'gentlemen', and against the background of trees and vegetation he looked like a fairy-tale gnome. A horrible green hat was pulled low over his monkey-muzzled face, and a torn raincoat wrapped his body like a bundle of rags. He didn't look as though he possessed twenty shillings.

'All right, twenty-five, Mr Lehman.'

'Twenty-five! Just what does the old boy think he's up to?' John Cain frowned slightly, glancing at his catalogue and the pencilled notes in its margin. 'Lot One Hundred and Nine – four mountaineering books.' That was the *First over Everest*, the two Kingdon-Wards, and a limited edition on British rock-climbing called *The Grey Boulders*. They had only reached a fiver in the sale, and twenty-five was absurd. Neither Roach nor Lehman would have a customer to pay that sort of money for them.

'Thirty-two!' No, it wasn't just absurd, it was quite crazy. Roach and Lehman were enemies, of course, carrying the scars of some trivial, unsatisfactory deal down through the years, but now they were just throwing money at each other for spite. That had to be it. At the very outside the lot was worth twelve, and he had marked that figure in his catalogue.

'Thirty-five!' All the same, why should he, or anybody else, worry if two vindictive old idiots wanted to cut their own throats? John looked at Peter Burton of the Chancery Bookshop, and grinned. The more Roach and Lehman fought over the lot, the more pickings there would be for the rest of them. Thirty-five against five already meant a very nice dividend indeed. The sale itself had been a wash-out – too few books among too many dealers – but this was making it a worth-while day.

'Thirty-eight!' From far down the drive he could hear the sound of lorries and porters' barrows. The furniture boys had settled their affairs, divided the spoils, and were loading up. They would have conducted their Ring in a comfortable warm van, he thought sadly. Not like the poor booksellers standing out in the cold. Grey dealers' faces, longing for town. Burton beside him smiling slightly, and probably gloating at the thought of his cut. Jack Goldsmith in tweeds, trying to look like a country gentleman and failing miserably. Sommers of the Ace Press with an expression of complete bewilderment on his thin, sick face. Bill Callaghan considering old men's mania. They had all stopped bidding long ago and were staring at Roach and Lehman.

'Forty pounds.' Roach raised his hand slightly. His face and eyes were almost hidden by his terrible hat, but he seemed to know exactly what he was doing. As always, John was struck by the strangeness of his voice. It had a marked cockney accent, but sounded false; as though the accent were put there to conceal an education he wanted to forget.

'Very well, guineas, Mr Goldsmith.' John looked across at Lehman, and he knew that this would be his last bid. The man's expression had been tense a moment ago, but it was quite blank now, apart from a slight air of smugness. Lehman hadn't wanted the books himself. He wasn't a specialist dealer in sporting subjects, and would have no customer to pay twenty pounds for them. He had known that Roach wanted them, though. Somehow, through some little, tortuous channel, he'd known that, and he'd driven old Roach up to the last gasp, the final level, but now he was finished. John watched him pull a cigarette from a crumpled packet and turn away, as though the whole business had become distasteful to him.

'Thank you, Sam. Forty-two pounds we are bid for Lot One

Hundred and Nine, Mr Roach, and it is against you. Would you like to increase on that figure?' Jack Goldsmith beamed on Roach like a wicked uncle persuading a nephew to spend all the contents of his money-box on a single trashy toy. He thought the man was probably out of his mind, and the thought amused him. All the same, there was a slight sense of anxiety behind the amusement. Old Roach had been in the trade a long time, and was supposed to know his business. Was there perhaps something about that lot they'd missed – something special about one of those books which made it valuable? Goldsmith hated the thought of missing anything. He was seventy-eight years old, with forty thousand pounds' worth of stock in the basement of his Chelsea shop, but the thought of a good buy slipping through his fingers unnoticed was a constant nightmare that troubled his sleep; rows and rows and miles and miles of books running away into other people's shops and catalogues, and not a single volume for poor old Jack Goldsmith.

But no, it was impossible; he'd checked carefully enough. He always checked carefully. There was no interesting inscription in any of those books to give it an inflated value. The Kingdon-Wards were in pretty poor condition and worth three at the outside; the *First over Everest*, say two; twelve was the best *Grey Boulders* had ever fetched. Roach was just a senile old fool, and Lehman had put him up for the hell of it. If he wanted to throw good money about, that was his affair. He bowed politely to Roach's forty-three pounds, glanced at Lehman, and then made a note in his pocket-book.

'Well, gentlemen, that seems to be the last of them, and now for our little financial settlement. As I make it, Mr Burton owes the Ring thirteen pounds, Mr Callaghan twenty-eight ten, Mr Roach – ' Like furtive gamblers they gathered round him and settled up; slips of ownership for those who paid, and a handful of notes for the rest. Everything was most satisfactory. The books had barely fetched a hundred in the sale, but they had trebled that figure.

'Well, Johnnie, I showed him, didn't I? I showed that bastard

Sam Lehman where he got off.' Roach crossed to John Cain and his little monkey face was a mixture of malice and good humour. When he smiled, a single gold tooth lit up his mouth like a lamp in a dark cavern.

'I don't think you showed him up, Mr Roach. I think you just made a bloody fool of yourself.' John didn't smile back. Though he and Roach had been friends for years, there was so much age difference between them that he still used the formal 'Mister'.

'No, Sam didn't want those books at all. He was just putting you up, and he stopped exactly when he knew he'd gone far enough. He's the one who should be laughing, not you. I'm not trying to tell you your business, and you're supposed to be a specialist in sporting books. All I know is that lot wasn't worth twenty, let alone forty-three. What happened to you just now? Did you go crazy and chuck good money away for the sake of beating Lehman?'

'Do you think that, John? Do you really think I'm crazy?' Roach shook his head sadly. 'Like the rest of 'em, you think I'm a senile old fool who doesn't know his business, and paid over the odds to spite Sam Lehman. Oh, I don't like him, that's true enough. Did I tell you what he did to me once? He had a copy of a nice book, but it was no good: there was a plate missing. He knew I had a copy too, so he asks me to send it to him on approval. It came back by return of post with a note saying that it was imperfect and lacked an illustration. The bastard had cut my plate out to make up his own copy.'

'Yes, I know all that. Lehman cuts a page out of a book, so you cut off your nose to spite him. Forty-three pounds you paid, just to spite him.' They were back in the house now, waiting for a porter to fetch Roach's lot. It must have been a nice house once, John thought: a warm, sunny house, with happy people and good furniture, and a nice little library. Now it looked like a battlefield, with the carpets tied up in rolls, and furniture being carried out to the waiting vans, and the library shelves empty. The last owner seemed to have been an invalid or a cripple, for there was a kind of sliding lift attached to the staircase. Somebody had bought that for three pounds, he remembered. Anyway, it didn't matter any more.

The owner was dead now, and estate duties had taken just too much. Soon the old house would be pulled down to make room for flats or offices.

'Oh, no, son, I didn't cut off my nose to spite Mr Lehman.' Roach's voice was like an old blunt saw hacking its way through rotten timber. 'Sam made me pay too much for that lot, but even at forty-three it's going to show me a profit – a damn fine profit.' He broke off as a porter came towards them.

'Yes, that's right, George, a hundred and nine it is. Thanks very much.' He handed the man half a crown and took the parcel from him, grinning up at John.

'Tell you what, son. You run me home in that nice motor-car of yours, and we'll have a cup of tea. Then I'll tell you a very funny story.' He swung the books up into the crook of his arm and, look-ing like one of Miss Blyton's gnomes, scurried to the door.

★ ★ ★

Roach lived in a side street at the south end of Clapham Common, and from the outside the house looked like a slum. The stucco of the porch was cracked and scarred, the paint was peel-ing, and the windows hadn't been cleaned for years. As he pushed open the door, they were greeted by a strong smell of dirty dishes, rotten timber, and damp. John walked carefully behind him down the passage, feeling the floorboards sink slightly under his feet, as though at any moment they might give way and hurl him into the basement. At the end of the passage Roach motioned him to a door on the right and turned into a small, grimy kitchen.

But if the rest of the house had been left to filth and decay, his workroom, library, or office was not. The floor was covered with highly polished linoleum, steel filing-cabinets stood by door and window, and there was a big electric typewriter on the light oak desk. On every wall there were books, thousands of books, neatly shelved and divided into subjects and sub-headings. In the spine of each volume had been placed a slip of paper giving details of its purchase and what it might be expected to sell for. John raised his eyebrows slightly as he looked at one or two of those slips. Roach placed a high value on his stock, it seemed. The prices were very steep indeed.

All the same, it was a nice stock: mainly sporting subjects, but there was a good section on early aviation too. If the old boy sold less than half of it at a reasonable figure, he could live in comfort for his few remaining years. As it was, he lived in a slum and worked like a black, running from shop to shop and auction to auction, and from time to time issuing catalogues to libraries and collectors which were so highly priced that he was probably lucky to sell a quarter of the items listed.

Not that John found this surprising. When you'd been as long in the trade as old Roach or Jack Goldsmith, books became a craze, an obsession, and you didn't really want to sell them. Money values changed, stocks and shares altered, and only books mattered to them and gave them security. Long rows of polished volumes stretching away under the light, the feel of a lovely binding, and the fun of finding a bargain. A tray of rubbish on a barrow or in a junk shop, and among the rubbish a grey, dust-stained volume which might – just might. . . . And as you handled it, and tried to remember what you knew or had read about it, you might hear a little voice saying, 'Buy me.'

Yes, he thought, it was a great life, if you didn't starve at it. All the same – he shook his head sadly at the parcel on the desk – there was no fun there, and no bargain. The four books it contained were common and well known. Even the most desperate collector would be ashamed to pay twenty for them.

'Well, here we are, Johnnie. Tea's up.' Roach came into the room and laid two steaming mugs on the desk. He made tea by the simple expedient of tipping leaves, condensed milk, and water into a kettle and bringing the lot to the boil. The liquid in the mugs looked and tasted like tar.

'Cheers!' He raised his hand in a mock toast and drank the horrible brew with every appearance of satisfaction.

'Now, let's have a look at my purchases, shall we?' He untied the knot and rolled up the string neatly for future use. 'And here's a little present for you, John. You've been very good to me in the past, running me out to sales in your car, so take these three, with my compliments. They're not much, but you should get a few quid for them.'

'Yes, you really are cracked, aren't you?' John frowned at the two Kingdon-Wards and the *First over Everest*. 'You really want me to have these? That means that you've paid forty-three pounds for a book which isn't worth twelve.'

'Yes, perhaps it does, son.' Roach pulled a tin of tobacco out of his drawer and rolled himself a cigarette. He talked with it in his mouth, the paper sticking to his lower lip like a growth.

'Yes, perhaps I did,' he said. 'But I still want you to have these three. They're no use to me, you see. I just had to buy 'em with the lot. Look at the shelves on your right. I've got two copies of *Land of the Blue Poppy* already, and three of *Plant Hunter in Tibet*. Maybe five of the *Everest*. What do I want more for?'

'Then you really did pay all that money just for this.' John stared at the remaining book in Roach's hand: a slim octavo volume bound in blue vellum, with an embossed crest on the cover made up from the design of an ice-axe and a climbing-rope. 'Just what's so special about it?'

'I don't know, Johnnie, I really haven't the slightest idea, but there's something special, all right – to one person anyway.' Roach pushed the book across to him. 'Just you have a look and try to tell me.'

'Thanks.' John tilted it to the light, and looked casually at the cover. He'd never actually handled a copy of *Grey Boulders* before, but he felt he knew all he needed to know about it from catalogues and auction records. A Trefoil Press edition on British climbs and climbers, published in 1910, with facsimile signatures of various personalities of the period on the fly-leaf. The edition had been limited to one hundred copies and sold to private subscribers by the publishers. He opened it almost idly and glanced at the list of signatures. Among them he could make out the names of Whymper, Mummery, and Owen Glyn-Jones.

Yes, a nice book, but not all that nice. The print was too ornate for one thing, and the thick, hand-made paper had lost its creaminess and was showing signs of 'foxing'. He turned through the pages and looked at the illustrations: photographs of moustached gentlemen wearing Sherlock Holmes costumes, standing roped together on ledges, pinnacles, and in dank drain-like gullies. There were captions beneath each picture giving notes on the climb and climbers. The Abrahams brothers on Scafell Pike, Jones negotiating the Tower Ridge on Ben Nevis, and a bearded clergyman raising a bottle to his lips before attempting to scale the Napes Needle. 'A friend in need is a friend indeed', ran the legend beneath that one.

'Well, I've looked,' he said, 'and there's nothing special about it that I can see.' John closed the book and pushed it away from him.

'Personally if I wanted to buy vellum, I'd much sooner have a nice Rackham.'

'Yes, I suppose you would, son, but you'd be wrong, you know, very wrong.' Roach's cigarette was stained a horrible brown now, and it danced up and down at the end of his lip.

'I was wrong too once, you know. Years ago, before I started to specialize, I made a bad mistake. I bought a first edition of *Wuthering Heights* for ten shillings, and I didn't know what it was. I thought it was just a nice Brontë three-decker, and I sold it to an American dealer – Paul Lascombe of Richmond, Virginia, it was – for a fiver. A month later I heard he had refused three thousand dollars for it.' His thin, old man's hand reached out and the fingers ran up and down the cover of the book. There was something very sensual about the motion.

'But I'm not making another mistake,' he said. 'No, not with this baby. I don't know why, but it's worth a lot of money to the right person. I wouldn't sell it to you for a hundred, John.'

'You mean you think you can find a customer for it? If you do, he'll have to be as mad as you are.' John forced himself to drink a little of the tea. Old Roach really was round the bend, he thought. There was no sense in him at all. The idea of any customer paying that money was just a pipe-dream. Yes, living alone as he did, with only books for companions, told in the end. There were no relatives or even close friends, and nobody knew a thing about his background. He must be getting on for eighty, and his brain was running down. They'd have to put him into a home if things went on like this.

'If you've got anybody who'll pay what you did for the book, I'd hang on to him like grim death,' he said.

'Oh, I'll hang on to him, son, you can rely on that.' A senile chuckle broke from Roach's lips without disturbing the cigarette. 'One has to hang on to good customers in my type of business – purely catalogue and postal trade. It's different for you with your nice bright shop, of course. You meet people, don't you? They come in and browse, and talk to you, and sometimes they buy books, or order them. There's a personal relationship, in fact. A poor old sod like me with just a typewriter to rely on never sees his customers, and I've got to keep them happy by results. They're just names on a mailing list, and if I don't get them what they want, they leave me.' He slipped a sheet of headed paper into the typewriter as he spoke, and finished his tea.

'And now, Johnnie, you'll have to leave me, I'm afraid. I won't say business is brisk, but I've got a lot of work to do.'

'So soon!' John grinned ruefully. 'But what about the funny story you promised to tell me in return for a lift home?'

'Oh, that! Let it wait a few days, son. You see, at the moment, I'm not quite sure how it finishes. And as for the lift, you've been paid well enough: two nice Kingdon-Wards, and the *Everest*. Don't sell them for less than a tenner. Now, be off with you.' His old, shifty eyes watched John Cain walk out of the door, and then he turned to the typewriter.

'Ref. your permanent inquiry,' he wrote. 'I have a good copy of the book in hand – Limitation number, 68. My price including postage is – ' He paused for a moment, dragging on his cigarette stub, and smiling slightly. Then he wrote 'one hundred pounds'.

'Well, what is it?' he said when he had finished, and once again his hand ran across the blue covers in that oddly caressing motion.

'Just what is your secret, I wonder?' Now that he was alone his voice sounded quite different. All the cockney accent had left it, and it was a cultured, almost academic voice.

'You're an ordinary, dull book, and I thought I knew everything about you. So what is it, my dear? What makes you worth that kind of money?' He leaned back in his chair, and seemed to be thinking about nothing at all, though his eyes remained fixed on the book in front of him. He was almost asleep when the doorbell rang, and with shuffling, old man's footsteps he got up to answer it.

★   ★   ★

John Cain didn't see or even think about Roach for the next two days, till a harassed film-set designer named Fred Lacey rang him up about a set of books on Regency costume. Lacey was a short, fat, jolly-looking man on the surface, but his body concealed an aching soul. He was either without work or up to his eyes in it, and everything he did was in a hurry.

'No, no, no, no, no, Mr Cain.' The voice came sharp and gasping over the phone, as though its owner had been running.

'No, that's no good to me at all – no good whatsoever. I realize you can get a set by advertising in your trade paper, but that takes ten days. If I'm to have those drawings in on time, I must have a copy of Tut-tut-tutter – ' he made a noise like a motor cycle starting up, and then brought out ' – Townsend's *Costume* by tomorrow.

'But please try and get me one, Mr Cain. I've been a good customer in the past, I think, and I'm relying on you to help me. This job is really most important to me.' He didn't sound like a customer so much as a prisoner begging for life before some Oriental despot.

'I'll do my best, Mr Lacey, but I can't promise anything. Townsend is pretty hard to find these days, but if I have any luck I'll ring you back.' John replaced the phone quickly, before another breathless outburst, and stood considering for a moment. The books would be hard to come by, but Lacey was a good customer and worth taking trouble for. It would be nice to do him a favour, and there should be a set somewhere in London.

Yes, he'd seen one not so long ago, he seemed to remember. Five slim, folio volumes bound in green cloth with scarlet labels, lying on somebody's shelf, or in somebody's window: Townsend's *History of Fashion, 1832*, which could save Mr Lacey from a spell of unemployment, and bring himself a nice little profit.

But just where had they been? He leaned back against his desk, seeing a picture of the books quite clearly, but not being able to place them. For a moment he considered phoning one or two likely dealers, and then the idea of Roach came into his mind. Roach wouldn't have a set himself, of course, for he specialized purely in sporting and aeronautical books, and Townsend was right outside his province or interest. All the same, if they were in a London shop, Roach would have noted the fact. His memory for books was like a computing machine, and two-thirds of his time was spent in wandering from shop to shop in the hope of finding something in his own field.

Damn Roach, though! The old idiot ran to an electric type-writer, and a modern duplicator, but no telephone. If he was going to get any help from Roach, he'd have to call round at his house. And why not? It was Wednesday, early-closing day, and his assistant, a slow-witted but very honest girl of fifteen, was perfectly capable of taking care of any passing customers. He handed her the keys and went out.

It was nice to be out of the shop for a while. Nice to smell fresh air and petrol fumes instead of the sickly smell of leather bindings, and dust, and polish. A nice morning, too: early April, with spring coming up in the trees, and the gas-holders looming on the horizon like ships. The kind of morning that made you want to drive on without purpose, or sail away anywhere and forget all about the trade, and catalogues, and bindings, and little whispered conversations of shady deals; nice just to drive.

But soon he was there; Clapham Common, with children playing football on the worn grass, and the town sloping away to Lavender Hill, with the identical, smoke-blackened houses looking almost pleasant in the sun. He sighed slightly as he got out of the car and walked up the steps to Roach's chipped and battered doorway.

'What a life,' he thought suddenly. 'What a rotten, wasted life!'

Roach had been in the trade for at least thirty years, but there were rumours that he'd once been something else; a university professor or lecturer who had made a bad mistake and been forced to pay for it, was the general opinion. In any case, and whatever the truth, there was something very sad about Roach. The man lived quite alone, without even a woman to clean for him, and there was not a single person in the world who really cared if he lived or died. Apart from his books and his mouldering ruin of a house, he had nothing. Soon he would die, and then the Council would condemn his house and tear it down, and the Public Trustee would have his books, for it was unlikely that he had even made a will. Then, one day, the books would be put up for auction, the 'boys' would make a killing, and the work of half a lifetime would go for nothing, or next to nothing.

Still, the old boy wasn't dead yet. He lifted the old-fashioned bell-pull beside the door, hearing no sound from inside the house, though, as if in answer, a motor cycle started explosively down the street. On the pavement two ragged children stopped and stared gravely up at him. The bell must be out of order, he thought, and knocked hard on the door. As he did so, it opened slightly. Old Roach had left it unlocked, then. Probably he'd nipped out to do some shopping. Once he'd told him that he never even had a bottle of milk delivered. John considered for a second, and then decided to go in and wait. The piercing stares of the children were becoming an embarrassment.

As he pushed open the door and stepped into the passage, the smell of the house wrapped him round like a blanket; dirt, dry rot, and stale greens mingling with an atmosphere that was made up of despair and neglect. Once again he walked cautiously down the corridor, feeling the boards twist and sink under his feet as he did so. It was the first time he had been in the house alone and, though he would never have admitted it to himself, he didn't like the feeling. If Mr Lacey got a copy of Townsend he would have to pay well for it, he decided.

But at least the workroom at the end of the corridor was as clean and efficient as ever. The curtains were drawn, but the window behind them must have been open, for they swayed slightly in the breeze. He looked around, staring across the room, and watching the thin gleams of sunlight mottling the books, and the steel filing-cabinets, and the . . .

'Oh, so you are in,' he said, seeing Roach standing on his right by the far bookcase.

'Didn't you hear me knock? I rang as well, but your bell seems to be out of order.' He smiled slightly as Roach started to turn towards him, and then stopped smiling. There was something unnatural about the way Roach turned; a very slow turn, as though it were a breath of air rather than muscle that was moving his body.

'I called to ask you if – ' He began to say, and then he didn't say anything, for it really was the air that moved him. Roach's feet were off the ground, and above the grinning gargoyle of his face a length of rope held him to the ceiling.

Two

'DON'T worry, it was suicide all right, Mr Cain. There's no doubt about that whatsoever.' Detective Sergeant James Manners leaned gracefully forward across his desk and smiled. He had a very bright, flashing smile, and his hair might have been plastered down with shoe-polish. Though he wasn't fat, he looked as sleek as a sea-lion, and you felt that if you pricked him he might burst.

'No, it's a week since your friend Roach died, and we see no reason to doubt that he killed himself. Our investigations have been pretty thorough, and the inquest is a foregone conclusion. On the day of that Highgate sale he was in a most unbalanced frame of mind; you and several of your colleagues agreed on that. He was a very old, rather unhappy man, living alone. The rope he used had been in his possession for years; you bore that out, I think, Mr Cain.'

'Yes, that's right. He collected relics and souvenirs of famous mountaineers, and that rope was the pride of his collection. It had once been used by George Mallory.'

'Mallory?' Manners frowned slightly. 'Oh yes, the Everest man. Chap who gave his reasons for climbing a mountain as merely "because it's there". Supposed to be clever, but I can never see why. "Why did you break into that bank, Bill Sykes?" "Because it was there, Your Honour."' He permitted himself another flashing smile.

'No, you can put your mind at rest, Mr Cain. Roach was an old, lonely man, and by all accounts he'd acted very strangely at that sale. Paid far more for a lot than it was worth, for instance. When you left him that evening, he may well have started to think that his mind was cracking up, and decided to make an end of it. He fixes a rope to the ceiling joist with a hook, and makes a pile of books which can be kicked from under him. That's about all there is to it. Very typical with old people living alone, I'm afraid. We get cases every other day.'

'Yes, I suppose so.' John looked away from Manners's compla-
cent smile, and he seemed to be back in Roach's room with the
glinting sunlight drifting through the curtains, and the thing twisting on its rope like a rag doll. And then his thoughts drifted farther
back still to the day of the sale, and Roach dismissing him and
turning eagerly to his typewriter.

'All the same,' he said, 'when I left him that evening he didn't
behave like a man who was planning to kill himself.'

'I'm sure he didn't, sir, but have you personally met many sui-
cides? And who knows what went on in his mind after you left?
That was at six o'clock, I think, and the medical evidence shows he
died about nine. A lot can happen in three hours.' The sergeant's
voice was still polite, but he was beginning to get bored with Cain's
suspicions.

'And if you'll take my advice, Mr Cain, don't even consider the
idea of foul play. We found not the slightest suspicion of it, and
if we had done – ' He broke off for a second and pulled open a
drawer of his desk.

'If we had the least idea that Roach was murdered, then I'm
afraid that you'd be under lock and key at this moment.'

'I!' John flushed slightly. 'But why? I was very fond of old Roach.
You mean just because I was with him on the evening he died?'

'Because you were with him, sir – because you found him –
because you are the only person who had a real reason for wishing
him dead; as far as we know that is.' He watched the bewilderment
on John's face and then slid a sheet of thick creamy paper across
the desk. 'Because of this, sir.'

'Good God!' As he read through it, the paper seemed to twist
and blur under John's eyes. 'But he never told me – he never gave
me a hint that he'd done this.'

'I'm quite sure he didn't, Mr Cain, but that's Roach's will all
right; all nice and legal and witnessed by his bank three weeks ago.
You're his executor and sole heir, and the estate includes a couple
of hundred pounds, the leasehold of his house, and what I understand is a pretty valuable collection of books.

'And I can't see any reason why we shouldn't let you inspect your property as soon as you like, Mr Cain. It's a bit irregular of course, but I'll take a chance for once. There's no doubt what the verdict at the inquest will be, and the bank doesn't anticipate any bother about proving the will. Don't sell anything till you get probate of course, or you'll have me in trouble. My congratulations, sir, and here is the key.' He handed it to John and then eased back his chair.

'Apart from the body, I think you'll find that everything is just as it was when you were last there.' He held out his hand and his smile flickered over John as though he had just given him the key to the bank of England.

'And now, Mr Cain, I'm afraid I've got quite a lot of work to do, and I'm sure you'll want to examine your inheritance. Goodbye to you.' He opened the door, watched John walk down the passage, and then moved back to his desk and lifted the house telephone.

'That you, inspector?' he said. 'Manners here, sir, and I've just had a chat with friend Cain. Yes, I gave him the key, as you suggested, and that should put an end to his ideas about murder, I think. No, he wouldn't have the guts to kill anybody himself, and it was suicide all right. Should we close the file now?

'Thank you, sir. Yes, that is still a point isn't it.' He frowned as he listened to the voice on the phone.

'No, we've checked with the Records Office, but it's no use at all. Apart from the fact that he had used a false name for at least thirty years, we've not the slightest idea who Roach really was.'

★ ★ ★

But Manners was wrong, everything wasn't just where it had been. One thing was missing.

John sat before Roach's desk, and he'd been there for hours. The cigarette tray was piled high with stubs, and all around him lay the litter of Roach's papers and record books. They told him nothing, or next to nothing. Nothing about the man's past or background, nothing about his fears or hopes or private feelings. Just records of business transactions stretching back across the years: quotation cards, order forms, and invoices. 'Dear Sirs, We can offer the following – ', 'Thank you for your order, but I regret the book is sold – ', 'Please send the copy of Greener's *Gun and its Development*, as kindly quoted – '

Yes, such a lot of correspondence: letters to suppliers, and offers to customers, and enquiries to dealers, but not one single letter from a friend or relative. Piles of catalogues neatly marked for reference, and lists of clients with their special interests beside them: 'Sir Charles Longden – anything on antique pistols and rifles'; 'Chief Librarian, University of Northern California – all on American Mountaineering'; 'L. K. Wilkes Esq. – back numbers of Rock and Fell Club journal'. Nothing which told him about Roach as a man, or why he had died on the end of Mallory's rope.

But Sergeant Manners probably knew his job. Roach was old and possibly unbalanced, and only he, John Cain, had had a motive for killing him. With Roach's death he was probably five thousand pounds the richer, so why should he complain? Roach had killed himself all right.

All the same, he had to be sure. He got up and walked slowly along the shelves of books, checking each title against the big bound catalogue written in Roach's neat hand, with date of purchase, price paid, and price hoped for entered against it. Here and there an item had been crossed out, and date and sum realized put in the margin. Everything in order, all books present and correct or accounted for. All except one book.

Very carefully he looked round the room, and then he went out and searched the rest of the house. He didn't enjoy that much. Roach might have been an efficient business man, but the squalor he lived in was indescribable; broken furniture, carpets mouldering with damp and dirt, and a lavatory pan that had probably been leaking for years. Every drawer and cupboard he opened looked as though it might contain some damp, toad-like creature which would close round his wrist with soft, fungoid hands.

But at last his search was finished, and he went back to the office and tried to marshal his thoughts. Roach had probably killed himself, but there was still a mystery to be cleared up; for something had been taken from Roach at about the time he died. He had last seen Roach sitting beside his typewriter, and just in front of him was a copy of *Grey Boulders*. There was no copy in the house now.

He leaned back in his chair, concentrating hard, and pulling at a cigarette. He had left Roach just after six, and he had died about nine. The local post offices shut at six sharp. He couldn't have posted the book that night, so somebody must have collected it. Was it possible that somebody might have killed for it?

But just what was there about the book to make it important? A rather pretentious volume of reminiscences written about people who had probably all died years ago. A book of which the top value was no more than twelve pounds, but for which an old, experienced and very astute dealer had paid forty-three, and claimed he could sell at a profit.

Yes, he would like to know the name of a customer who would pay that sort of money for *Grey Boulders*. Plots of long-forgotten detective stories started to run through his head: wills hidden away in bindings, incriminating documents stitched in among the pages, a map showing the way to buried treasure. Had there been something special about that one copy which Roach had somehow spotted?

He thought of the sale and the knock-out afterwards. Everybody grinning and gaping as the price went up and up, and they knew the lot would bring a dividend past their wildest dreams, while Roach nodded his head, and Lehman kept raising a not-too-clean finger. Yes, Lehman must have known something about that book, it seemed. He'd never have risked going to forty-two if he weren't sure that Roach would top his bid. Sam Lehman had known all right. Horrid Sam with his cunning, pointed face, and long yellow teeth protruding over the lip. A face like an illustration from a child's book of animal stories in which the characters have human clothes and characteristics; 'Mister Rat, the dealer,' with a great, grey tail poking out through his baggy breeches. Yes, it would be interesting to have a word with 'good old Sam Lehman', as he called himself.

'Flaxman – nine-four-five-four.' The voice at the end of the line was thick and muddy, and sounded as though the mouth that produced it was full of food, which was probably the case. Lehman would have shut his shop by now, and be sitting down to high tea in the room above. John could imagine what it would be. Sam had cast off his religious principles years ago, and to drive home the point favoured strongly Gentile and unclean dishes: bacon and sausage, and strips of fat pork washed down with scalding tea.

'Johnnie boy, Johnnie Cain, how nice of you to ring me.' The voice changed to a peal of delight, as though the call was the one thing that made his day.

'And what can I do for you, Johnnie? Want to sell me something, eh? Bought something good? Plenty of cash here, boy, and you know I always pay well for anything in my line.'

'I've heard that, Sam.' Lehman was one of the worst payers in the trade, and John had never been able to discover exactly what his 'line' was. On the surface he dealt in literature and history, but there were rumours that he had another and more profitable interest. At the back of his shop there was a little room which only the most favoured customers were allowed to enter. Rather nervous and grey-faced customers on the whole, who went in furtively and came out bearing well wrapped and unlabelled parcels, which they returned a week or so later – poorer but certainly wiser men. If rumours were true, Lehman ran a choice and expensive library of smut which enabled him to keep a young mistress, spend long week-ends at Brighton and Eastbourne, and gamble industriously but unprofitably at the Dogs.

'No, Sam, I haven't bought anything much lately,' he said. 'All the same, I think I may have something to interest you. You see I've just been left about three thousand books, and I wondered if – '

'Left, left is it! Three thousand left to you, is it!' The voice rose to a near scream of delight.

'And so you want me to help sort 'em out for you, boy. It's nice that, Johnnie. Nice to hear of a young man pocketing his pride, and asking an old stager like me to lend a hand. I appreciate it, and of course you know you can trust me. Yes, I pay a fair price for anything I can use. Ask anyone in the trade, and you'll hear the same thing – "Good old Sam Lehman pays a fair price," they'll say.

'And just what are those books, boy, and who left 'em to you? Some rich uncle perhaps, with a taste for leather bindings?'

'No, not a relative, Sam, and there aren't many bindings among them. They're a few aeronautical books, and a lot on sporting subjects.'

'Sporting books, oh!' For a second the voice was slightly guarded, and John sensed that Lehman took the word 'sporting' as a reference to the rumoured erotica in his back room. Then it changed back to excitement again.

'You mean – you don't mean old Roach's books? He left 'em to you, did he, Johnnie? Well, well, the poor, old devil! He had no family, so he left 'em to you, just because you ran him round to the sales once in a while.' He paused for a moment, and John heard a clink of china as though Lehman were considering his next move and fortifying himself with a swig of tea.

'And who better should he leave 'em to, Johnnie? Oh, yes, I know what a good friend you were to old Roach – very, very kind to him you were – and I'm delighted to hear he made you his heir. Why, I was just saying to my young lady the other day, "He's a good friend to Mr Roach is Johnnie Cain," I said.' He sounded like a schoolmaster complimenting a favoured pupil on a well deserved prize.

'And you're doing the right thing, son, coming to me. Roach would have liked the thought of us two going through his stock together. Oh, yes, we've had our differences in the past – who hasn't? – but deep down we were as close as brothers. Like all the trade, he knew he could trust me with his last farthing.

'By the way, Johnnie, did you hear what Jack Goldsmith said about me at the last Rare Bookdealers' Dinner – "Our toast, gentlemen, is Mr Sam Lehman of Viaduct Books," he said. "As we can see, the years have left some stains and dust-marks on old Sam's cover, but inside he is as mint and clean as ever." How the boys laughed and cheered!'

'Yes, I was there.' John winced slightly at the horrible memory.

'And now, Sam, let's get down to business, shall we? I know you'd give your eye-teeth to have a look at those books. Roach told me himself that you almost forced your way into his house on a couple of occasions.' He ignored the squeal of indignation at the end of the line and went on.

'Well, you can look at them all right, but first I want a little information from you. Just what was so special about that copy of *Grey Boulders* the other day?'

'The *Grey Boulders*? Oh, yes, I remember. You were at the sale, weren't you?' Lehman sounded very guarded now, and his voice had lost all forced friendliness.

'Just what do you want to know about it, Johnnie? I should have thought a look at *Auction Records* or *Book Prices Current* would tell you all you needed to know.'

'No, Sam, they don't tell me anything at all. What I want to know is this. You and old Roach were supposed to know your business, so what happened to you? Why did you bid over forty pounds for a book which never fetched more than twelve?'

'All right, Johnnie, I'll tell you.' Lehman had paused slightly, but now his words came out in a rush. 'If you promise to let me have some of Roach's books cheap, I'll tell you. I thought the old fool had got his hands on a Kamtsen.'

'Kamtsen?' John vaguely remembered the Yiddish word. It could roughly be translated as 'hoarder'.

'That's right, boy, a Kamtsen; the crazy collector we dreams about, like we dreams of finding a First Folio, or a Gutenberg Bible; the man who craves for a certain book, and doesn't care what he pays or where it comes from. You often find them in the picture trade; some mad bastard buying a stolen canvas he can never show, but gloats over in a cellar. It's a form of sickness, I suppose, but a bloody useful form if you get hold of a rich one.'

'Yes, I know it. Even a poor one is pretty good.' John remembered a customer of his own, a retired clerk living on a pittance, who bought copies of a certain local print at five guineas a time, and was quite frank about his motive. 'I can't bear the thought of anyone else having them, Mr Cain.'

'But *Grey Boulders* isn't the kind of book to attract a nut, Sam,' he said. 'It's far too general for one thing. If it was merely about one climber, like Mallory, say, and appealed to somebody's hero-worship, then I can imagine – '

'Listen to me, Johnnie. I'm no psychologist, boy, I'm just a poor, bloody bookseller, and I'm telling you what happened.' A chair creaked loudly, as though Lehman was moving his bulk into a more comfortable position.

'About four months ago old Roach came into my shop and bought a copy of *Grey Boulders*. Beat me down, he did, and only paid a tenner, but that's not important. What interested me was that I heard later he'd also bought one from the Sheridan Book-shop, and another from Fred Jackson. That made me prick up my ears and keep my eyes open, as you can imagine.'

'Yes, I can imagine it, Sam.' As he listened a horrible picture flicked through John's mind: an enormous grey rat with Lehman's face nosing for scraps in a dark alley.

'Sure I did. I talked to dealers, and to porters at the sale rooms, and I looked in magazines. Old Roach had been advertising for that book in the *London News*, *Sporting Life*, and half a dozen others. During the last year or, so he'd bought over thirty copies; that's getting on for a third of the whole edition.'

'The devil he had! And you checked that, Sam?'

'I checked it all right, Johnnie, and when I saw there was a copy going at Highgate, I thought the time had come to risk a little money. Forty guineas I decided to put up for that lot. If Roach overbid me, then all the boys would have a nice dividend; if not, if I bought the book, then I might just get my teeth into Roach's Kamtsen."

'Sorry, Sam, I'm not with you.'

'You should be, boy, if you only use your head a little. These people aren't normal, you know. They crave for the things they collect, like a drug addict craves for dope. Suppose that this man of Roach's had told him to bid up to thirty for the book, and Roach lost it. The man would be upset, I think. He'd sit at home and feel as though he'd lost his wife or mother, and decide he should have offered more. His crazy mind would tell him that the book was worth every penny he had in the bank. Then he'd start to make a few inquiries, and he'd hear that the copy had been bought by Mister Sam Lehman of the Viaduct Bookshop. And so he'd come to me, and I'd have a share in Roach's hoarder. You see the idea now?'

'Yes, I see it,' John said, but what he really saw was how it might have ended: Roach sitting alone in his room with the copy of *Grey Boulders* beside him, waiting for a customer to call. And then the doorbell had rung, and he had got up to admit that customer.

And the customer might have been a poor man, and Roach might have been greedy and asked more than he could afford. Then perhaps the sick mind had considered what was in his wallet, and what the bank manager had written, and how much the wife owed on hire-purchase, and known he couldn't pay that price. But all the time his eyes had flickered at the little blue-bound book which glinted on the table like the Holy Grail, and told him he had to have it.

Then, as he looked, the urge and craving might have turned to action; a blow on the head, leaving a bruise so slight that it had faded before the police doctor came on the scene, and Roach's little body twisting on a rope.

Impossible – or was it? John knew a lot about collectors' urges, and nothing would surprise him any more. One example in particular came to mind; a big, florid, happy man who collected a pleasant though common series of books known as *Britain's Heritage*. Yes, he'd been happy all right. 'I've got number sixteen at last, and that leaves twelve to go. And you think you can lay your hands on number thirty-nine for me? Thank you, Mr Cain, thank you very much indeed. I only need eleven to complete the set then.' His eyes had sparkled like diamonds at the news.

And then one day they'd met in the street, and the man wasn't florid, and his eyes didn't sparkle at all. He'd lost weight, too, and his suit hung round him like sacking. He wasn't happy any more. 'Yes,' he said, 'I've got the lot now – the whole series. I can relax, can't I, Mr Cain?' What he really meant was that all the fun had gone out of his life.

Yes, collectors were a strange breed, and if Roach had found one who was not only strange, but ruthless too; if he'd driven him too far – yes, then he might have found a killer.

'Thanks for telling me, Sam,' he said. 'Yes, that's just what I wanted to know, and you can have the first refusal on any of Roach's books I decide to sell. I'll let you know when to come round and look at them.

'What's that? Oh, yes, of course, a promise is a promise. And, as everyone in the trade will tell you, good old Johnnie Cain is as straight and true as a ramrod.' He replaced the phone before Lehman could reply, and stepped out of the box. A plan of campaign was starting to form in his head, but he wanted some advice first. He walked past Roach's house and climbed into his car.

★ ★ ★

'Get out of the way, Cain.' Mrs Beatrice Budd – Bee to her friends, Beelzebub to her enemies, who were many – lifted a heavy, leather-bound volume from the pile on her table, and hurled it across the shop. It twisted past John like a boomerang, and fell into a crate labelled 'Robinson'. She was about fifty-five, looked like somebody's very nice maiden aunt, and was rumoured to be rich. John had no reason to doubt this, for he knew a good deal about her business.

Like everybody else in the trade Mrs Budd woke up each morning and considered what she might sell to America, but her considerations had a money-spinning gimmick. Whilst almost everyone else had single, expensive items in mind, she sold in bulk and she sold cheap.

At every local auction where cheap lots were going she would be found, bidding for the books nobody else wanted, providing she got them for a song, and selling them the same day, for across the Atlantic she had found an octopus who devoured everything she could give him: an aged dealer in Chicago who rejoiced in the name of 'Miles of Books Robinson', and who had hit on the idea that people will buy almost anything provided it is cheap – really cheap. Surprising enough the theory had paid off, and both Bee and Mr Robinson were waxing fat.

Crash! Another heavy tome shot into the hamper. Bee was feed-

ing her octopus well, it seemed. That morning she had bought
over two thousand tatty volumes for less than ten pounds, and was
busy sorting the sheep from the real goats. Two-thirds of them
would be crated off to Robinson, and the stickers would droop on
her own untidy shelves marked a shilling or sixpence.

'Yes, of course I knew about old Roach's death. Been expecting
it for years.' She paused in her labours for a moment and regarded
John with little, bulging eyes that reminded him of a Pekingese.

'Didn't know he'd made a will in your favour, though; bloody
old fool. Yes, off to Chicago with you, my dear.' She snorted loudly
and hurled a volume of Churchill's War Memoirs at the crate.

'And you think it may not have been suicide, do you, Cain?
Bloody fool yourself then. The poor old devil had enough on his
conscience, by all accounts. At the same time, I suppose there
might still be people about who felt that they had a reason for killing him.' She frowned slightly.

'But this nonsense of some mad collector killing him for a climbing book, you can forget that right away. Maybe that rat Lehman
is right and Roach did have a crazy customer, but so what? If you
saw some of the loonies who browse in here on a Saturday, nothing would surprise you. They're not killers, though.'

'Bee!' With great difficulty John broke into her torrent of
speech. 'I'm not with you at all. You say that Roach had a reason
for suicide, that there might be people who would like to kill him?
Well, for God's sake what was it? What had he done?'

'You mean you don't know?' Her face crinkled with disbelief.
'He didn't tell you? He left you all his books and his money, but he
didn't tell you who he really was? Wait here for a moment.' She
padded out into her back room, and returned with a slim quarto
book in her hand.

'Does the name K. 105 mean anything to you, or are you too
young to remember?'

'Yes, I remember. I read it up some time ago. It was an airship,
wasn't it? It crashed on its maiden flight, and killed everyone on
board.'

'That's right, Cain, it crashed.' She laid the book on the desk and flicked it open. 'This is the man who got the blame for the crash. Look for yourself.'

'Thanks.' John craned forward to look at the bound volume of an aeronautical magazine, dated 1921, and laid open at a photograph of a man leaning against a hangar wall. 'Mr J. R. Bruce, designer of the Airship K. 105,' read the caption under it, but even with the age difference, even with the hat drawn down over the forehead, he could recognize that face.

'Roach! That's who he was?'

'That's right. Roach – I still can't think of him by his real name – designed that airship, and it crashed. The court of inquiry found him responsible, and he was pilloried in the Press, as happened to Thomas Bouch who designed the Tay bridge. After a time he couldn't stand it, and made himself disappear. Changed his name to Roach and became a book runner, going from shop to shop and buying and selling at a few pennies' profit. He must have had quite a flair for it, and soon built up a mailing list; aeronautical stuff at first, and then sporting books as well. I only found out who he was by chance when I was going through these magazines.'

'And you never told him you knew?' For the first time in his life John seemed to have a true picture of Roach. That was the reason for the forced accent, the loneliness, and the hat which he wore pulled down even in his house. Even after thirty years that burning airship might have troubled his dreams and given him a reason for suicide.

'No, I didn't tell him. I didn't tell anyone, though I'm not saying I wouldn't have spread it around if Roach had crossed me at the sales.' Mrs Budd grinned, but John knew that she meant exactly what she said.

'But the point is that what I've shown you should prove that Roach had a perfectly good reason for suicide, and if the coppers say that's what happened, they're probably right. An efficient bunch on the whole, though a pack of busy-bodies at times. Why, only last week a couple walked in here to check if I had any stolen library books on the shelves. They went out with a flea in their ears, I can tell you.'

'I'm sure they did, Bee.' John grinned back at her, but though he liked Bee Budd, and hated Sam Lehman, it was Sam he trusted, not her. Roach's death had nothing to do with any long-forgotten air disaster, but with a book. A little vellum-bound book that had lain innocently on Roach's desk and then disappeared. A book which might hide a secret in the same way that the magazine had told Bee who Roach really was. He had another theory to go on now, as well as the mad collector idea, or something hidden in one special copy.

'And now, Cain, I'm going to kick you out. Stan Robinson's a good customer, and he likes his stuff on time.' Her voice cut into his thoughts.

'And don't worry any more about Roach. He killed himself all right, and that book had nothing to do with it. Of course, if you're still not satisfied, there's a very easy way to prove it.' She smiled at the bewilderment on his face.

'Yes, of course there is. Roach had a mailing list, hadn't he? Well, use it. Go and quote a copy of *Grey Boulders* to every name on his list. Then, if there is a murderer, you'll bring him back to you like a homing pigeon.' As though dismissing the matter from her mind she turned and began to rummage among the piled books on the table.

* * *

It takes a long time to build up a good mailing list, but Roach had had thirty years. John read on through the thick, black ledgers which contained the names of his clients with their special wants and interests beside them, and he wondered if one of those names might belong to a killer. Though he had no facts to go on, he was quite certain that there was a killer. Whatever the police or Mrs Budd might say, whatever Roach had on his conscience, he wasn't the kind of man to kill himself; not on that night, anyway. On the night of the Highgate sale he'd been very happy and excited.

He leaned back in his chair, staring across the small, brightly lit office, and he tried to imagine how it might have been if his theory was correct. Roach was quite well known among collectors of sporting books, and one day he might have received a postcard or letter – 'I should be glad if you would offer me any copies of *Grey Boulders* which may come your way.' The writer could have been either a stranger or a customer who had been on his list for years.

In any case it was probable that Roach would have at least one copy of the book in stock, and he would have quoted it, and received cash with order by return of post. And so he would have offered this prompt payer more copies, possibly quoting from other dealers' stock, and each offer would have been accepted.

Then slowly the price would have gone up. John had no illusions about Roach's character. If he thought he had a customer with a compulsive urge he would have put on the screws like a Levantine usurer.

Yes, the price would have gone up and up, and in a way he would have been justified. The edition was limited to a hundred copies, and a good quarter of these would be safely stored away in libraries and climbing clubs. Each copy he had supplied made the book a little scarcer and more valuable, and finally he might have started to believe it was worth what he charged.

Then, exactly a week ago, that long-suffering customer would have come into the room to collect his final purchase. John wondered how much Roach had asked for it. He'd paid the Ring forty-three, so sixty would have been a reasonable sum. And as he heard the figure, the man might not have believed it at first. Then, as Roach explained the working of the knock-out, the word 'swindler' could have come to his lips, and annoyance turned to blind fury.

Yes, it might have been like that, though all he really knew was that a certain book had been taken from Roach's house, that Roach had been buying up copies of that book at absurd prices, that Roach was not the kind of man to kill himself. Still, as Bee Budd had told him, there was an easy way to prove his theory. He leaned forward again and began to study the mailing lists still more closely. Amongst all those names there could be the one he wanted, and he was going to try to bring its owner into the light. He picked up a pen and started work.

The first thing was to separate the sheep from the goats. Though Roach had been a specialist, he had dealt in every type of sporting book, and customers whose interests were stated as archery, cricket, big game hunting, or any form of sport except mountaineering could be discounted. Also those not resident in England. After an hour he had forty-eight names and addresses written down in front of him.

And most of those could be cut out, of course. The Bishop of Tonbridge Wells, for example – His Honour Judge Reeves – Sir Stephen Lent, who was the chairman of Allied Engineering Combines, he seemed to remember. No, they damned well couldn't be cut out. A bishop, a judge, or an industrialist might have a sick mania for collecting, or a secret to be hidden, as easily as anybody else. There were forty-eight names, and he would quote to all of them. Forty-seven would look at the card, raise their eyebrows at the price, and throw it aside, but one might be shocked enough to come into the open. Always assuming, of course, that Roach had put the name of that rather special customer on his list.

But anyway it was worth a try. He slipped one of Roach's quotation cards in the typewriter and started work, leaving the bill-head as it was, but adding his own name and 'Successor to', and putting in his own telephone number. Then he described the goods he was pretending to sell, the bait which might bring a murderer into the open. 'We can offer a fine copy of the Trefoil Press edition of *Grey Boulders*. Edition limited to 100, our copy numbered – ' No, he couldn't remember the number of Roach's copy, so he typed in '50' at random. As he did so he glanced at his watch. Nearly nine o'clock, and the central post office had a collection at midnight. If he worked hard he might just make it. The big electric typewriter whirred and clicked under his fingers, the desk lamp lit him up like a figure on a stage set, the rows of books seemed to frown down on him as though he were disturbing their sleep. He concentrated on nothing except filling in those impersonal cards which might bring him face to face with a killer. '*Grey Boulders* – Trefoil Press Edition – Our copy number, 50 – Price £43 – *Grey Boulders* – Trefoil Press – Price £43. – '

But at last he was finished, and the cards lay in front of him stamped and addressed and ready for posting. He slipped a rubber band round them and got up. Once they were in the box the trap would be sprung. If his hunch were right, somebody who thought he was safe might get an unpleasant surprise with the morning's mail.

Three

By nine thirty that morning a number of people had read John's quotation, and most of them had dismissed it with sadness or the contempt it deserved.

His Honour Judge Reeves, for example, looked at it on the way to court, and at first he was pleased. He had wanted a copy of the book for some time, and felt grateful to Roach's successor for remembering him. Then his eyes fell on the price and they seemed to draw back into his head. Old offenders knew that cold, shrunken look well, and the most courageous of them blanched before it. A hard man, the judge, hard on the bench, and hard on the rocks too; the Reeves Chimney on Scafell, and Reeves's Ruin in the Grampians, testified to his prowess.

'A fool,' he muttered to himself. 'A fool or a knave!' He threw the offending piece of paper on to the floor of the car and, without acknowledging his chauffeur's salute, hurried up the Old Bailey steps to pass a remarkably savage sentence on a seventy-year-old bigamist.

★　★　★

Herbert Skinner, Bishop of Tonbridge Wells, was slightly more charitable.

'Poor old Roach,' he said mildly, glancing at the card propped up against his coffee cup. 'His business has fallen into very grasping or ignorant hands, I'm afraid.' He felt slightly put out, as though somebody took him for a sucker, but his expression didn't and couldn't alter. At the age of twenty-five he had had the misfortune to fall off the West Wall of Pillar Rock, and the resulting thirty-mile-an-hour collision between his face and the scree below had left him with a grinning, rigid mask which could have done gargoyle-duty in his own cathedral.

'Still, one must be charitable,' he thought, getting up from the breakfast table and crossing to a desk. 'Perhaps this man, Cain, is merely ignorant, or has made a typing error.' He drew a circle round the offending price, and wrote: 'Is this intended as a jest?' Then he signed 'Herbert Tonbridge' with a flourish, and slipped the card into an envelope.

'Yes, one should be charitable and give people the benefit of the doubt,' he thought complacently, and glanced at his watch. 'All the same, if the fellow really meant what he wrote, it was an insult to his own intelligence. Forty-three pounds indeed!' Anger rose like a pressure gauge as he considered the enormity of the figure. The Diocesan Conference was due to start in five minutes, and though they didn't know it, his assembled clerics were in for a pretty thin time.

★ ★ ★

Unlike the bishop, Dr W. P. W. Wright, M.B.E. (awarded for services to British sport), was not charitable at all. After a single brief glance the card had been condemned, torn in halves by strong white fingers, and hurled aside as though it were a particularly disgusting object, while a loud, scornful laugh rang across the consulting room. At the end of the room two crushed receptionists glanced timidly at each other.

'Oh dear,' they thought. 'Doctor's in a mood again. It's going to be one of the bad days, is it?' Still more timidly they listened to the voice of their employer muttering angrily to herself.

'The man's nothing but a bloody swindler who ought to be horse-whipped,' said Winifred Wright, President of the Ladies' Alpine Club.

★ ★ ★

But if the bishop, the judge and the doctor had dismissed the quotation, there were others who did not.

Mr Philip Reade, Keeper of the Metropolitan Library, for instance, studied it very carefully, and then called for his assistant.

'Tell me, Miss Sss- Sims,' he said, stuttering slightly, which he always did when something bothered him. 'Isn't this the book which we had that – that – '

'Which we had that unpleasantness about.' Miss Sims finished the sentence for him.

'Yes, sir, that's it all right: the Trefoil edition of *Grey Boulders*.' She picked up the card and squinted at it through her glasses.

'But this is quite absurd. Forty-three pounds indeed! The average price in auction records is only ten. I know Mr Roach always tried to charge up to the hilt, but this man who has taken over his business appears – '

'Yeee-Yes, I know that, and I think there must be some mistake. I feel that he must have been dooo-doing a number of quotations, and mixed it up with another book.' As the theory came to him Reade's speech started to improve.

'Yes, of course, that's what happened, he's mixed it up with something else. We'd better get through to him at once, and ask for the proper price. Tell him what happened to our copy. It might make him a little more sympathetic. A nasty business that, Miss Sims. A very nasty business indeed!'

★ ★ ★

But less than a mile away from the Metropolitan Library the book had already found a buyer. Sir Stephen Lent, Chairman of Allied Engineering, glanced at the card, and hardly noticed the price. Once there had been a time when, however rich he was, he would have fought over shillings, but now he was too old and tired to bargain. Forty-three was absurd, of course – this fellow was trying it on – but he wouldn't argue with him. He wanted a copy of *Grey Boulders*, and here was one for sale.

'I wonder if you'd mind doing me a favour, my dear,' he said, smiling at his niece Julia across the vast mahogany table which seemed ridiculous for two people.

'Could you run out to Clapham this morning, and pick a book up for me? The man won't find many buyers at his price, but I don't want to lose it.'

'Yes, of course I can.' Julia reached across for the card and smiled back at him. She had lived with Stephen Lent since her mother died two years ago, and they were very fond of each other. They also pitied each other.

Julia pitied her uncle because, though on paper he was still chairman of Allied Engineering, it was only on paper. Since that last illness he had been forced to delegate authority and give up control of the firm, and the firm was the only thing that mattered to him. He was like a dry husk now, without hope or interest.

On his part Lent pitied Julia because she was too rich; one of the richest women in England, probably, since he had made over that last block of shares to her in the hope of avoiding death duties, and keeping the firm in the family. He respected money and possessions himself, almost loved them in fact, but without that love they were dangerous things.

Wealth – real wealth, not just thousands, but hundreds of thousands – could make a young woman turn sour before her time, and he dreaded that happening to Julia. Yes, unless you loved them for themselves, money and power could be very frightening. The knowledge that the fairy godmother was always waiting at the end of the telephone to provide a dozen minks, a yacht, and a string of well-born suitors was frightening.

He'd seen the results himself a score of times. Women who wore the best clothes in the world, who had the best beauty treatment in the world and the best make-up in the world, staring out over blue seas with the faces of old, frightened whores. Women whose thoughts were probably always the same – 'Is it the real thing this time? Does he love me this time? Has it happened at last, or is it just the cheque book – always the cheque book? Oh God, if only I were sure that he even liked me for myself!'

'Yes, poor, little Julia,' he thought. 'It will be a good thing if she marries soon. Marries anyone, however old or unattractive, providing he is half as rich as she is – providing he can give her some security.'

'Oh, it's that book, is it, Uncle?' Her voice broke into his thoughts, and she frowned slightly as she looked at the card. 'The one you lost.'

'Yes, the book that was lost, stolen, or strayed – most probably borrowed and not returned.' Lent gave a cynical, old man's smile.

'It's a strange thing, you know, but people who are on the whole perfectly honest – who would not for a second consider keeping a wallet they found in the street – think nothing of borrowing a book and failing to return it.' He shook his head sadly.

'And there's a family reason why we should have a copy of *Grey Boulders*, you know. It contains quite a lot of material on your grandfather and my father. Yes, they were great figures in their day, Bill and Hal, the Lent Brothers. Not known to the public, of course, like Mummery and Whymper with their spectacular Alpine ascents, but they did some wonderful climbs in Wales and Scotland; great pioneers. We should have a copy of the book as a record of them.

'And now, Julie, I think I'll get along to the office. Peter Trew is an efficient, loyal fellow, but he can't carry the whole concern single-handed.' Sir Stephen pulled himself up from the chair, and walked slowly to the door. Since that last stroke he had to walk slowly, and Julia knew how much he hated it.

'Goodbye, Uncle,' she said, watching those dragging footsteps that only will-power kept moving. 'But please take it easy. You know what the doctors said.

'And don't worry about the book. I'll go round for it now and bring it to the office. Give me something useful to do for a change. God knows I need it.' She gave a little, bitter smile which showed no pleasure, and followed him out of the room.

* * *

John had sent out forty-eight quotation cards, and at least five people had noted their contents with anger, bewilderment, or acceptance. A sixth person noted it with sheer, murderous rage.

The man sat at a table which was littered with books and papers, and the remains of his breakfast, and the room around him might have been designed and decorated by a maniac. The man himself was an unpleasant sight, too. He wore a suit of surprisingly vulgar pyjamas, open at the top to show a mat of reddish hair, and his face bore an expression of almost inhuman arrogance. A big, heavy man, sixteen stone if an ounce, and all of it bone and muscle; an ill-tempered man who could become a very bad enemy on very small provocation.

At first he had merely glanced at the card, and then his eyes fell on the serial number of the copy, and something rather horrible started to happen to him. If possible his enormous body seemed to grow still bigger, his tanned, leathery face glowed like a lamp, and his throat and neck muscles flexed like cords. Finally a noise that was made up of astonishment, rage, and near apoplexy burst from his lips.

'My God!' he said, when at last he regained the power of speech. 'Oh, my God, just you wait till I get my hands on you, Mr Cain!'

Four

FIVE minutes after John had opened his shop that morning he received a phone call from the Metropolitan Library. It was a long, tortuous call with Mr Reade's voice slurring and stuttering at the end of the line, but when he finally replaced the receiver his eyes were very thoughtful. Part of his theory was beginning to come up, it seemed. Somebody with a very strange or abnormal mind was interested in *Grey Boulders*.

He arranged the outside shelves as usual, answered a couple of letters, and then handed over the shop to his assistant and went round to Clapham. At least half his quotations would have been delivered by now, and it took him quite an effort to go. Roach's house possessed no telephone, and anybody who wanted to contact him there would have to call personally. The memory of Roach's grinning face above that knotted rope was suddenly very close to him.

Still, he had other work to do. Roach's books were his now, and he would have to sort them out properly. Most of them were too specialized for a shop, and all were too highly priced for a quick sale. If he wanted to sell them quickly, he would have to alter the markings. He pulled out the catalogue and four copies of *Auction Records*, and started to make a list.

It was a lovely day again, with spring sunlight peering in through the dusty windows, and as he worked his thoughts about Roach's death began to change. He wanted them to change, his mind made them change, because he wanted to stay alive.

Yes, it was probably suicide, he thought, as he sat there working at something he both loved doing and understood how to do. Even with what Reade and Lehman had told him, the fact that a man had an obsession with a certain book didn't make him a murderer. Besides, the disappearance of that last copy could easily be explained: a dishonest policeman with an interest in mountaineer-

40

ing literature slipping it under his coat as he went out, perhaps.

Yes, he thought, but he knew he was lying to himself. Bee Budd was right, and Sergeant Manners knew his job. After all, what had he to go on? And he was the only person to benefit from Roach's death. He'd been a damned fool, and he should have stuck to his own business. If his theory was false, those cards would make him the laughing stock of a large number of collectors and librarians. If correct, he'd left himself wide open to a person who had killed before and would probably have no hesitation in killing again. You fool, he thought. You poor, silly fool. Why didn't you mind your own business and let the police mind theirs? He bent over the list again, and then sat up with a jerk. The little rusty bell in the passage was ringing.

Very, very slowly, John Cain got up and walked to the door, and he more than half hoped that his caller would turn out to be somebody completely innocent and unimportant – a man to read the meter, a postman, a fellow bookseller come for pickings. He pulled it open, and looked at one of the most beautiful girls he had ever seen.

'Good morning. Mr Cain, is it?' Julia Lent smiled up at him from the step. She wore a Balmain suit, and the car parked behind her had probably cost more than John could hope to save in a lifetime.

'I've come about a book you were kind enough to offer my uncle, Sir Stephen Lent; the title is *Grey Boulders*.'

'Oh yes, of course.' John had seen that smiling face in a score of the glossier magazines, usually accompanied by a chinless scion of Scottish nobility named Jimmy Stuart-Vale. For a second he struggled to collect his thoughts, and then stood aside in the doorway.

'Would you come in please, Miss Lent.'

'If you wish, but I can easily write a cheque out here.' Julia hesitated a little. She saw a man in his early thirties, pale and stooping, but still rather attractive. His house, on the other hand, with its chipped paint and stucco, and the dark cavern of a hall behind him, was like a threat. She drew back slightly, seeing the plea in his eyes, and then pushed the thought away. This man wasn't after her honour, but merely her money. She followed him along the passage to Roach's office.

'No, there's no need to wrap the book up, Mr Cain. I'll just take it as it is. Forty-three pounds, wasn't it?' She pulled a cheque book from her bag.

'Miss Lent, just a minute, please.' John's eyes studied her as he spoke. 'Would you listen to me before you write that out?' No, he decided, this girl wasn't a murderer, or the representative of a murderer. People like the Lents didn't kill for what they wanted. With control of Allied Engineering behind them they didn't have to. They merely took a cheque like the one she was holding, drawn on a very select private bank, and signed it.

'Thank you,' he said. 'And now please don't think I'm impertinent, but if I may I'd like to ask you a question. Just why are you, or rather your uncle, so keen to have the book?'

'Why!' Julia flushed deeply, and she looked even better when she was angry. 'I'm very sorry, Mr Cain, but I do think that's an impertinent question. You quoted the book to my uncle, and he wants to buy it. He is prepared to pay what I understand is well above the market price. That is all that should concern you. Now may I have the book, please?'

'Miss Lent.' John's eyes pleaded with her. 'Please be patient, this is terribly important to me. As it happens I know a little about your uncle. He's been collecting sporting books for years and I would have thought he had a copy already. Also, though he's a very rich man, he's a collector as well, and however rich they are, collectors hate to pay more than the fair market price. It's a point of honour with them because it spoils the fun of the thing, like cheating at a game where there's no money involved. So why does your uncle want another copy of the book, and why did he accept my quite absurd pricing?'

'Yes, he told me it was absurd.' Julia smiled slightly and relaxed. The man was obviously just an amiable idiot with too much curiosity.

'Until a few years ago, my uncle was a very hard businessman, and he would have beaten you down to a proper figure within minutes. I'm quite sure of that, Mr Cain. Two years back he had a stroke, though, and it's left him old and tired and without the energy to bother about little things any more. He wanted a copy of the book because it has some family material in it. His father and my grandfather were quite famous climbers in their day. I seem to remember there was a picture of them in *Grey Boulders*, taken just before my grandfather was killed on a mountain in Scotland. We had a copy, of course, but he said it had been lost or stolen.'

'Stolen!' Something like a little spring seemed to click home in John's head. 'And have you any idea by whom? Oh, I'm sorry, that's a silly question.'

He broke off for a moment, knowing she must think him crazy, but having to concentrate. A hundred copies of the book had been printed, and Roach had bought a third of them. Then Roach's last copy had disappeared at about the time he died, Sir Stephen Lent's copy had been stolen, and the copy in the Metropolitan Library –

The memory of Mr Reade's voice on the phone ran through his head like a gramophone record – 'Oh, we know that those sort of things happen in the public or free libraries, Mr Cain, but not in the Metropolitan. All our members are so carefully screened, you see; three references, a degree from a reputable university, and proof of financial status, before one is even allowed to join. As I said to my assistant, "these things may take place in the British Museum Reading Room or even the London Library, but never in the Metropolitan."

'And it was the way the book had been treated that was so horrible, Mr Cain. This wasn't just the work of a thief removing plates to make up an imperfect copy of his own. It had been slashed and torn as though a maniac had done it, as though somebody bore the book a personal grudge.'

'A maniac!' John whispered the word aloud, for that was the most probable explanation, it seemed. Somebody who felt he had a secret hidden in the book would merely have removed the incriminating pages. A hard-working maniac too. An old dealer had been killed for the book, a millionaire had been robbed of it, and a very swagger library had had its copy mutilated. He was

beginning to picture the kind of mind that was at work. Somebody who hoarded the books, but didn't want anybody else to
have them; an efficient somebody, though. The Metropolitan was
a reference, not a lending, library, and no one was allowed to take
a book from the premises. It would have been very hard to steal
that copy, but quite simple to deface it. He began to feel a deep
dread at the thought of that crazed but efficient mind.

'Mr Cain – Mr Cain, are you all right?' He looked up with a jerk.
Julia Lent was staring at him, and there was a lot of concern in her
eyes.

'Yes, I'm all right. Just very sorry.' As he looked at her, he knew
that he wasn't all right at all. He was desperately lonely, and afraid,
and bewildered, and the one thing he wanted was an ally – somebody to talk to.

'Miss Lent,' he said, 'would you bear with me a little longer, and
let me tell you a story?' He smiled slightly. 'I expect it will either
make you very angry with me, or just think I'm mad.'

But when he had finished the girl wasn't angry, though he'd
told her that the book didn't exist and she'd come on a wild goose
chase; and she didn't seem to think he was mad. She just sat still,
watching him for a moment, and her thoughts might have been a
hundred miles away.

'Well, it seems to me that you're either a fool or a very brave
man, Mr Cain,' she said at last. 'People do kill themselves, people
mutilate books for spite, and people borrow books and fail to
return them, which is probably what happened to our copy. Everything may be pure coincidence, in fact.

'All the same, if you're right, if there is some insane collector
at work, then you've left yourself wide open, haven't you? The
moment he gets one of your cards, he'll know you suspect him,
and he won't like it at all. Why on earth didn't you just tell your
story to the police, and have done with it?' She listened to his
explanation and nodded.

'Yes, I suppose they would have laughed at you. After all, you've
got precious little to go on at the moment. I'd like to believe you
though, Mr Cain. It would be great fun to have a mystery to

unravel. Thanks.' She took the cigarette he held out and inhaled deeply.

'But perhaps I'm taking too much for granted. Did you really want my help when you told me about the book?'

'Yes, I'd like you to help all right.' John got up and stared out of the dusty window. The weather was breaking now, and there were grey clouds drifting up the river.

'In fact, I think you may be one of the few people who can help, Miss Lent. You see, assuming I'm not quite insane, and this person really exists, we're beginning to know something about him now. We know that he must have been in contact with Roach for several months, that he had access to your uncle's library, that he was a member or employee of the Metropolitan. We've got three trails to follow, and if you would, I'd like you to take the second. Find out the name of everybody who had the opportunity to take your uncle's copy, and I'll make inquiries at the Metropolitan. Then, if we find two names that match, we could be half way home.'

'Yes, I suppose we might be.' She considered for a moment, and then smiled and held out her hand. 'And if we're to be partners in crime, let's not be formal. My name is Julia.' Her hand was soft and warm, and full of the sort of confidence that money and breeding sometimes produce.

'Very well, John,' she said. 'We're in this together now, and let's go back to the beginning. Tell me everything you know about the book itself. It might give me a lead to the sort of person who wants it so desperately.'

* * *

She had gone at last, but he had an ally he knew he could rely on. They had arranged to meet that evening, and with any luck two names might fit together, and there would at least be a suspicion to go on.

Yes, Julia would make a good ally, he thought, remembering the way she had walked confidently across the rotten boards in the passage, as though challenging them to give way under her, and the way her car had shot professionally forward with barely a sound. He watched it round the bend, and then looked down with a jerk.

'Nime o' Kine?' A bullet-headed urchin was scowling up at him, and had just given his jacket a hearty tug.

'Gotter letter for you,' he said, and handed John a crumpled envelope with his name typed across it above Roach's address, but no civility of Mister or Esquire. John didn't open it at once, but looked down at the bearer. The boy was about twelve, but his face might have belonged to a middle-aged and very pompous man. The kind of boy who was destined to do well in any occupation that demanded a loud voice, push, and a burning desire to feather one's own nest; a scrap metal merchant, for instance, a fairground barker, or a local politician. Yes, he would go far in any of those fields.

'Who gave you this, son?' he asked.

'Didn't say 'is nime. Gent in the Park, it was. He stopped me and asked if I'd deliver it for 'im. Real gent he was.' There was a gleam of hero-worship in the little, pig-like eyes.

'Gimme five bob he did, and said you was to 'and over another ten when you got it, plus me bus fare. That comes to one and two return.'

'Did he indeed! Well, we'll see about that.' John frowned, and opened the envelope. It contained a single sheet of paper bearing the address of Vanessa Court, a block of flats in Kensington, and three lines of heavy typing.

'Your name is well chosen, Mr Cain,' he read, 'and you appear to be one of three things: a thief, a swindler, or a forger. Bring that book to me before twelve noon or take the consequences.' He couldn't make out the inked scribble under the message, but it might have been the signature of somebody named Golden God.

Five

VANESSA COURT stood at the top of Gloucester Road, Kensington, and from the outside it looked small, select, and very expensive. The hall inside bore out that impression too. Here there was no garish lighting, vulgar decoration, or carpet that held your feet like marshland, but plain, polished boards, heavy Victorian furniture, and curtains draped across the windows to shut out the day. People who had flats there obviously liked their privacy, and they would be the best people too. To get a tenancy in Vanessa Court would be no mere question of paying a premium or putting one's name down on a waiting list, but as difficult as joining an exclusive club.

All the same, the best people obviously had one 'dark horse', if not a raving lunatic, in their midst. The words of that insolent message seemed to burn before John's eyes as he walked across the hall. He remembered sending a card to Vanessa Court, but not the name of the person to whom it had been addressed. He was quite sure that he would be a very rum customer indeed; probably a dangerous one too.

There was no porter in the office, but a board marked the floors and flat numbers, and the lift gates were open. John stepped through them, and smoothly and silently the machinery carried him up to the second floor. He walked out into a small, dimly-lit passage with the door of Number Six straight in front of him.

And he wasn't frightened – not really frightened; though his palms were damp with sweat, and a little pulse beat in his forehead. The writer of that note couldn't be Roach's murderer. A murderer wouldn't have revealed himself like that. This was merely some unbalanced eccentric who thought he was being overcharged and enjoyed being insolent. All the same. . . . He suddenly decided that he wasn't just frightened; he was bloody terrified.

'Come in, the door is not locked.' It had swung open slightly at his knock and through the gap a voice rolled towards him; a loud, booming voice which might have come from the lips of an ogre. The hall inside was bare and untidy, with packing cases stacked against the walls, piles of newspapers, and what looked like sporting equipment hanging from pegs.

'In here, man, and quick about it. I don't like to be kept waiting.' Deep and domineering the voice rang out from a doorway at the side of the hall. He pushed open the door, and then gasped in astonishment.

For the room within was like a madman's horror, or a child's very bad dream. It was decorated with sporting trophies, African drums and devil masks, and outlandish primitive weapons. The curtains were drawn, but a row of lamps concealed in skulls, some animal, some human, provided ample illumination.

'Well, it's Mr Cain, I presume, and it's lucky for you that you decided to keep our appointment.' The rasping arrogance of the voice seemed to shake the entire building, and it contained both threat and sneer, as well as rank ill temper. Its owner was just like it. He lolled back in a chair with his feet propped up on a desk, and a lamp at his side lit him up like a television announcer. He had a flowing ginger moustache, an enormous bald head, and a smile which was one of the most disagreeable things John had ever seen. He looked as though he weighed about sixteen stone and was in the pink of condition.

'All the same, you haven't kept me waiting long which is one slight thing in your favour. Now let's have a look at you.' His great, ginger hand tilted the lamp at John.

'No, not a thief, I think. Not enough courage in your face to make you break in and steal anything. Merely the receiver of stolen property, or some poor dupe who has had it foisted on him in ignorance. Well, hand it over, man. Providing no damage has been done, I may just consider being lenient.'

'I don't know what the hell you're talking about.' John struggled to control the near hysteria in his voice. 'All I know is that I received an impertinent communication from this address, and have come for an explanation.'

'*You* have come for an explanation!' A dark, angry flush spread across the man's face, and his vast body seemed to swell and grow still bigger.

'You say that you don't know what I'm talking about! Well, let me remind you.' He picked up one of John's quotation cards and brandished it before him.

'Are you denying that you sent this?'

'No, I don't deny that.' John struggled to remember the names he had copied from Roach's mailing list. Vanessa Court was one address all right, but he couldn't recall any name that even vaguely resembled 'God'.

'I sent out several of those cards, but – '

'Oh you did, did you?' The man's expression changed from fury to contempt. 'Then that confirms my opinion. You aren't the thief, but merely the receiver. Somehow the book got into your hands, and when you saw the book-plate you realized you were on to a pretty good thing. Forty-three pounds is absurd for an ordinary copy of *Grey Boulders*, but not for that particular volume.' His hand crashed on the desk in emphasis.

'So you sat down, didn't you, Mr Cain, and wrote reports to people who might be expected to realize its importance. But you slipped up – you made a bad mistake. Your little, mean mind ran through the list of names and you typed them out automatically and without thinking. And one of those names happened to be mine. Yes, you're in the soup, aren't you, my friend?

'And now where is the book? If you've already sold it, things will go very hard with you.'

'No, I haven't sold it. But what about the book-plate? Just what is there about the plate that makes the book so special?' John was convinced he was dealing with a lunatic, but suddenly he was not afraid at all, only very interested. This was the first person who considered the book was worth a high price.

'What is there about the plate!' The effect of his question was extraordinary. A noise that was part curse, part groan burst from the man's lips, and his face glowed like a lamp bulb. For a moment he seemed in danger of a stroke.

'Mr Cain,' he said when at last he had recovered the power of speech, 'Mr Cain, for your own sake don't provoke me. I'm not a man who suffers either fools or insults gladly.

'You must know as well as I do what is so special about that copy, or you would never have offered it at that price. Number Fifty of the limited edition of *Grey Boulders* not only bears the facsimile signatures of Whymper, Mummery, the Abrahams brothers, and many of the rock-climbing personalities of their day, but it also bears the book-plate and signature of one of the greatest modern exponents of the sport. Yes, forty-three pounds seems very cheap to me for a copy associated with J. Moldon Mott.'

'It was your copy then?' As he heard the name a row of brightly jacketed books seemed to slide before John's eyes, and he knew who this ogre was. The books bore the imprint of a sound publishing house, and their format never varied. On each jacket the man stood against a jungle, desert, or mountain background, with groups of adoring natives around him, and usually he wore shorts and a sun-helmet, and there was a rifle or a coil of rope slung over his shoulder. *Mott's Wanderings in Central America*, the titles read, *With Mott across the Lost Kalahari*, *On the Track of the Abominable Snowman*, by J. Moldon Mott. There was also a highly sensational biography of Ghengis Khan entitled *The Scourge*, in which the author strongly identified himself with his hero. Yes, John had heard of Moldon Mott all right; part explorer and adventurer, part author, and by all accounts a very dangerous fellow indeed. There were several unpleasant stories about what had happened to people who crossed him.

'It was your copy and somebody stole it?'

'Most certainly someone stole it, Cain.' Mott's hands twisted together as though the thief's neck were already between them.

'Three or four months ago, when I was on that Borneo expedition you must have read about, some sneak thief broke into the flat. The fellow must have been a maniac, it seems, for he took nothing except that one volume. If he'd been a little more enterprising he could have got away with all my notes and diaries; quite priceless stuff.

'All the same, Cain, however trivial it is, I want that book back, and I want to find the thief. Nobody is going to rob me with impunity.' A rhinoceros-hide whip hung in the corner of the room, and Mott's eyes ran longingly over it.

'Well, out with it, man, I'm waiting. Just who sold it to you?'

But John didn't answer for a moment. This was the fourth copy they knew about, he thought. One had been mutilated, and three had been stolen – at least three – and at least one man had died because of them. Already he was beginning to reject the idea of a maniac. There was a cold-blooded planning about this business which didn't fit in with mania.

'Mr Mott,' he said at last, staring at the glowering face before him, 'I think I'd better put my cards on the table and tell you the truth. I never had a copy of *Grey Boulders*, and I merely quoted Number Fifty on the spur of the moment. You see, I'm trying to bring a killer into the open – '

★   ★   ★

'So, it seems that there are just three possibilities.' Mott's forehead worked up and down like a gorilla's as he concentrated. 'Your mad collector theory, which I don't dismiss, but don't set much store by either. The idea that there is one copy in existence which our murderer must get his hands on because it holds something either incriminating or of great value. And the theory that there is something special about the whole edition. Drink?'

'Thank you, I could do with one.' John watched him lumber across the room, and return with an amber bottle and two glasses.

'But this last theory, the one you seem to favour – that there is something special, some secret, hidden in the whole edition. Just what sort of thing could it be? Almost everyone mentioned in the book must be dead by now.' Memories of his brief inspection of the book in Roach's office ran through John's mind; pictures of climbers long dead, and descriptions of their feats. 'We ascended the Tower Ridge by the East Wall. Fifty feet above the first chimney the real difficulty begins, but the leader is aided by a small, grassy ledge which gives ample space for one person to belay – '

'We don't know that yet, do we?' Mott poured out two generous measures of whisky and pushed a glass across to John.

'All the same, I'm quite sure there is something, and we're going to find out what it is. You were very wise not to tell your theory to the police. On the whole they are intelligent men, but a problem like this would leave them standing. No, this needs a person of, not only great intelligence, but imagination too. Yes, Cain, you were in luck's way when you sent me that quotation. I intend to run down this thief and murderer.' He raised his hand with the gesture of a dictator silencing a cheering mob, and then drained his glass.

'No, no thanks, old boy, not yet. I'm a modest man, so keep your gratitude till we've unravelled the mystery.

'Interesting that old Stephen Lent should have had his copy stolen. With the army of servants they keep in that mausoleum of a house, it would be pretty difficult to get away with a match stick. I can imagine how much the old boy would want to replace his copy, though. His father and uncle, Hal and William, had almost a whole chapter devoted to themselves, I remember. Yes, a rum couple the Lent brothers seem to have been. Identical twins, and always climbed together; did some wonderful first ascents in their day. Then Hal fell off the Great Flake on Ben Gael and was killed. Brother William never climbed again after that; buried himself in a small firm his father had left him, and built it up into what it is today – Allied Engineering, one of the biggest concerns in the country.' Mott refilled their glasses, and leered at John like a rutting baboon.

'If you cut a dash with little Miss Julia and got your toe through that door, you'd be doing all right for yourself, my boy.'

'I dare say, but I can't see much possibility there.' John frowned and turned away from the grinning face.

'And just what do you think our plan of action should be?' He both resented Mott, and welcomed his intervention.

'*Our* plan, Cain, does not exist. Up to now you have behaved in the most foolhardy manner, and it's what I say that must go from now on. By all means check with Julia Lent for a connection between her uncle and the Metropolitan Library, but I doubt if you'll find one. This bird will have covered his tracks too well for that.' He pulled out a short, blackened pipe and proceeded to ram tobacco into the bowl.

'And, in a sense, this idea of your unpleasant colleague, Lehman, could be on the right lines. Roach may have found an unbalanced or crazy customer, but there is more to it than that. Perhaps the man was crazed because there was something in the book which terrified him, and perhaps he killed because Roach tried blackmail.'

'Blackmail! Sorry, I'm not with you.'

'No, I suppose not. I suppose you're still struggling to be loyal to your benefactor, all the same you must accept the facts.' Mott sounded like a schoolmaster explaining a simple point to a well-behaved but very dense pupil.

'Friend Roach is given an order to dig up any copies of *Grey Boulders* he can find. Well, after a time he becomes suspicious. He feels that he may not merely have a hoarder, a Kamtsen, as Lehman calls it, on his list, but something much more interesting. Somebody who wants those books, not to hoard and gloat over, but to destroy. Somebody who is frightened, in fact. Somebody who knows that, hidden away in the pages or plates of *Grey Boulders* is a piece of information which can hurt him.' The pipe was filled to his satisfaction now, and clouds of acrid smoke started to drift across the room.

'I met old Roach once or twice in the way of business, and I can imagine what he'd do, if he suspected anything like that. He'd search the book very carefully, and if he found something to get his teeth into, the idea of blackmail would come easily to his nasty little mind. – No, no, Cain, don't interrupt me.' Mott scowled as John tried to break in.

'I know what you're going to say. The book was published in 1910, and what possible threat could it contain now? All the same, the sins of the fathers are said to be visited on their children, aren't they? Whose father, I wonder? Who can have a little family secret hidden away in a book published fifty years ago?

'And, if a man like Roach can stumble on the truth in a few months, it shouldn't be difficult for somebody like – like – ' modesty prevented him from saying 'myself', so he compromised with – 'somebody of real intelligence to dig it out in a matter of hours.

'Yes, Cain, my first job will be to go through a copy of that book, and then I can get down to the real work. I'll try and meet you and the Lent girl this evening, and we can compare notes. You may find a link between the theft of her uncle's copy, the Metropolitan Library, and Roach's customers, though I doubt it. As I said before, this man has proved himself both intelligent and courageous so far, and I think he'll have concealed his identity.' As though concluding the interview, Mott got up and pushed back his chair.

'See you this evening then, old boy. That is, if you're still alive, of course.' He grinned and raised a great gnarled finger in warning.

'Oh, yes, Cain,' he said pleasantly. 'As the Bard has it – "by the pricking of my thumbs, something wicked this way comes" all right. If our killer really does exist, and has received one of your cards, then I think we can safely expect an attack on your life during the next few hours.'

Six

METEORITE HOUSE, Headquarters of Allied Engineering and its daughter companies, had few of the frills usually associated with big business. A squat, red-brick building, without Doric pillars or marble facing, it stood a little way back from the Embankment, as though slightly ashamed; a dowdy sister among its more splendid neighbours. Where the factories were concerned Stephen Lent spent money like water, but what he considered false show or unnecessary advertisement always brought a slight coldness into his face.

'I would ask you to remember that we are engineers first and businessmen afterwards,' he often remarked to his board of directors, which included an earl, two lords, and a retired admiral. 'Nor, gentlemen, are we in show business. The kind of publicity Allied requires comes from up-to-date plant, good labour relations, and customers' orders fulfilled dead on time and to the exact requirements. This building was good enough for my father who was the real founder of the firm, and I see no reason to squander money on it now.' Whatever dignitary had suggested the changes always looked away from that cold, wintry face.

For a moment Julia chatted to old Forest, the doorman, who seemed to have been standing in the same spot and in the same uniform since she was a child, and then walked up into the hall. As in the rest of the building, there was no fuss or pretence there. Three grim-faced old ladies sat behind reception desks, there was a long row of lifts and telephone booths, and only in the centre was there anything that hinted at ornament. A gigantic piece of blackened machinery towered to the ceiling: the Perseus Steam Hammer, designed by William Lent in 1912, and one of the main stepping-stones to their fortune.

'I'm sorry, Miss Julia, but Sir Stephen is engaged at the moment. He's with Mr Crawford of our Lancashire works.' Her uncle's secretary frowned up at her. She had the expression of an old, devoted sheepdog, and like most of the senior staff had been with the firm for years.

'And I do wish he wouldn't come in so often, Miss. Oh, we all love to see him, but since that last stroke it does seem dangerous. As I was saying to Mr Trew only yesterday – '

'And what were you saying to Mr Trew, Mary?' The man came almost silently into the room and smiled at them. He was middle-aged, medium sized and medium coloured, and wore his black coat and striped trousers like a uniform. Apart from his eyes, which were very keen and intelligent, nobody would have noticed him in a crowd.

'Hullo, Miss Julia,' he said. 'Don't you go paying any attention to Mary. She fusses over your uncle like an old hen. He may have had a stroke, but business is still his best tonic. We've been together a long time and I know him.'

'But come and wait in my room, will you? I don't think the Chief will be too long. That wretched fellow, Crawford, has fallen down on an order and is having a strip torn off his hide.' Peter Trew opened the door, and led her across to his own office: a very bare room with plain steel desks and hard chairs which might have belonged to a monk.

'Do sit down and make yourself comfortable, Miss Julia. A cigarette?' The case he held out to her was brass, and quite unfitted to a man who was almost the controlling brain in the organization.

'By the way, didn't I see your picture in the *Tatler* last week? With that chap Stuart-Vale, I think it was.'

'Yes, you could have done, Peter.' She accepted his light and leaned back as far as the chair would allow. 'You don't approve of Jimmy Vale, do you?'

'No, not really, I'm afraid, though of course it's none of my business. I think you could do much better, you know, Miss Julia.'

'Do you, Peter? How nice of you. But tell me something. Just why do you always call me *Miss* Julia? After all, I've known you since I was a child, and you're a director of the firm now; probably the only one that matters since Uncle was ill. It makes me feel rather like a barmaid.'

'Sorry, Miss Julia. I'd hate you to feel that, but I'm afraid I can't help it.' A little flicker of a smile ran across his face. 'Perhaps it's stupid of me, but I just can't think of you in any other way; just as I always think of your uncle as the Chief. You see, when one's whole life has been spent in working for the Lent family – '

'Yes, I know all that, but it's still stupid of you, Peter. It might have been all right once, but you're a very important and probably rich man now. Just what is your salary, by the way? At least twenty thousand a year, I imagine, so let's accept each other as equals.'

'Oh, no, I don't earn anything like that, Miss.' Trew's smile widened slightly.

'After the Chief's first illness the Board suggested twenty thousand, but I didn't accept it. After all, why take money from the firm and pay it straight over to the tax collector? I've no family to think of, and my own wants are simple. I don't entertain much either. We pay several sprigs of the nobility to take care of that side of the business.' He shrugged his shoulders and sat down facing her.

'No, my life is here, and I prefer to think of myself as just a company servant – which means a servant of your family, of course. I'm afraid you'll have to remain Miss Julia as far as I'm concerned.'

Trew stared round the office as he spoke, and he knew it was the truth. He wanted nothing else. Just to be the loyal and trusted servant, the steward with delegated power, was his ambition in life. Sitting in at a board meeting, not giving orders but passing them on. Looking along a row of self-important faces, and seeing them turn away as he stated that this or that was the policy of the firm; that was the way Sir Stephen wanted it, and so it would be. Pressing a switch on the intercom and sending fifty locomotives to Brazil, a floating crane to Nigeria, three generating plants to Sydney. Standing in front of a row of union officials and telling them what could be granted, and what was impossible; that the company had always kept faith with its employees, and if they wanted to remain on the pay-roll, they'd better keep faith with it.

And at the end of it all no reward or personal gain, except the pleasure of seeing Stephen Lent smile, and hearing his voice say, 'Thanks, Pete, I knew I could rely on you. I always know I can rely on you.'

'Very well, if that's the way you want it, I'll stay Miss Julia.' She smiled back at him. 'Your family and ours have worked together for a long time, haven't they, Peter?'

'A very long time, Miss. Three generations it must be now. My grandfather was your great-grandfather's foreman when he started the first forge down at Gravesend. My father was manager to your grandfather and great uncle. Now I'm with your uncle. As you say, a long time.'

'Yes, it certainly is.' Julia glanced at a photograph behind his desk, and considered the humble beginnings and what they had become. A scowling gentleman with a bowler hat and mutton-chop whiskers standing before a tarred shed, to thirteen factories in three continents, and mineral rights in half the globe.

'And I wonder what it was like in the beginning, Peter. My great-grandfather, for instance. Was he the old slave-driver he looks like in that picture?'

'I suppose so, Miss. By all accounts most of them were in those days. Hard on his sons too, I've heard. Said they had no interest in the firm, and would ruin it within five years of his death. Left some sort of clause in his will to stop that happening. Oh, excuse me a minute, will you, I've been expecting this call.' He lifted his ringing telephone, answered it briefly, and then put it down again after reeling off a string of figures with the speed of a computing machine. As she listened Julia realized that it was efficiency as well as loyalty that made Trew the most important cog in the business.

'And I wouldn't be surprised if the old boy wasn't right,' he said. 'From what my father told me, Mr Hal – that was your grandfather – and Mr William, his brother, didn't take much inter-est in work at first. Just drew on the profits, and spent their time in mountaineering and winter sports. Very famous they became, but it nearly broke the firm. Then Mr Hal was killed on a moun-tain in Scotland, and William never climbed again. Pulled himself together and got down to work. Turned out to be a fine engineer as well as a business man, too. The Perseus Hammer was one of his. I suppose we could call him the real founder of the company as it is today.'

'Yes, I suppose so.' Julia glanced at her watch. 'Do you think my uncle will be much longer, Peter?'

'I shouldn't think so, Miss. If it's urgent, of course, I'll ring through to his office and ask.'

'No, don't bother. It's not important – just about a book he asked me to pick up for him. He lost his own copy some time ago and wanted this one to replace it. It has some family history in it.'

'Yes, yes, I remember.' Trew frowned slightly. 'He mentioned something to me about it. A book on mountaineering called *Grey Hills*, wasn't it? He seemed upset at the time. Yes, that's right, Miss, *Grey Boulders* was the title. He hadn't looked at it for six months or so, and then when he wanted it it had gone. About a fortnight ago, that was.'

'Six months!' Julia's face dropped a little. In that time a great many people could have had the opportunity of taking the book. She didn't see much chance of telling John Cain anything useful.

'Yes, I think that's what he said. But here he is now.' Trew got up quickly as the door opened.

'Ah, there you are, my dear.' Stephen Lent came slowly into the room as a man must do when he has had two strokes in as many years, but he didn't look tired at all. Peter Trew seemed to be right: business was his best tonic.

'I hope Peter has been keeping you company. Thanks, son.' He lowered himself carefully into the chair that Trew pulled out for him, and beamed up at them.

'You must be very nice to our Peter, Julie. He's not only my right-hand man, but a sort of male nurse as well these days.

'Now, my dear, did you get it for me?'

'No, I didn't get it, Uncle.' She watched the little flicker of disappointment in his face, and felt some of it herself as she did so. Her own father had been killed in a motor smash when she was twelve, and though they'd never been close till recently, Stephen Lent had gone a long way to taking his place.

'You didn't! But, Julie, my dear, what happened? Surely he couldn't have sold it so soon?'

'No, no, he didn't sell it. Uncle, are you all right?' There was tiredness as well as disappointment in his face now, and the eyes seemed to be about to close.

'Yes, I'm all right, Julie – quite all right.' Lent shook his head as though to clear his thoughts.

'But what happened to the book? This man offered it to me this morning, so what's become of it? He must either still have it or have sold it.'

'No, I'm afraid it's not as simple as that, Uncle.' Julia had promised to keep John's theory to herself, but concern for her uncle made that promise seem unimportant now. He looked not only tired, but ill.

'You see a copy of the book was bought by a man called Roach, but he died and this John Cain took over his business – '

'Yes, yes, I know that.' Once again came a quick, impatient shake of the head. 'That was clear from the card heading. But what has happened to the book, Julia?'

'The book never really existed, Uncle. When Roach died his copy was stolen, and Cain thinks it had something to do with his death. He sent out a lot of quotation cards to try and bring the thief into the open.'

'To bring a thief into the open! Sorry, my dear, I just don't understand you.' Lent's face was exactly as she had seen it after that last stroke – grey, empty, and without character. The face of a child who has just seen a well-loved doll torn to pieces.

'I'll try to explain, Uncle. You see, during the last few months, Cain thinks that somebody has been buying up copies of *Grey Boulders*, and probably stealing them as well. There was also a library copy mutilated. He thinks there may be some pathological collector at work, a lunatic – Uncle, what is it?'

'A lunatic, eh!' A single sharp laugh broke from his lips. 'So, that's what he thinks, is it? Just a lunatic.' With a convulsive jerk he pushed back the chair and staggered to his feet, swaying slightly against the desk.

'Our friend Cain seems to be a smart man, my dear, but he's wrong, you know – terribly wrong.' The eyes were wide open now and they looked as though they'd seen through the gates of hell.

'Just a lunatic! Oh, Julie, my dear, if only he were right!' His face went completely blank, his knees buckled, and he slid forward towards the waiting arms of Peter Trew.

Seven

SIR STEPHEN LENT had had another stroke and been carried unconscious to his bed. Julia had listened to the doctors, and knew that this time it might be the end. John Cain had spent a fruitless afternoon searching the bookshops and libraries for copies of *Grey Boulders*. Mr Mott had not been idle.

The Trefoil Press had ceased as an independent concern years ago, but still existed as a prestige branch of the Henderson group of publishers, who from time to time issued an expensively got-up edition under its imprint. Within an hour of John Cain's leaving him, Mott marched through the portico of Henderson House, grinned horribly at the receptionist, and announced 'Mott for Heaven', in clear, ringing tones.

'You have no appointment, sir?' The girl had only been a few months with the firm, but already she fancied she could distinguish the sheep from the goats. Mott was clearly a goat: the possessor of some worthless, unpublishable manuscript bent on bothering their directors. A good two-thirds of her time was spent dealing with people who called without appointments, and above all things the directors must not be bothered by them. Quiet, anonymous men, they cowered away in their offices, screened from the public like Arabian Nights princesses. She smiled maliciously and lifted the house phone; in a moment she would send this unwelcome caller about his business. Then the smile left her face and was replaced by a look of astonishment.

'Will you go through, sir,' she said. 'The second door on the right.'

'Mr Moldon Mott! How nice of you to call and see us.' Stanley Heaven, chairman of Hendersons, twisted his foxy face into what he imagined was a beam of welcome.

'Yes. It's a great pleasure to meet you at last sir.' He fought back a yelp of pain as Mott took his hand in a bone-crushing grip.

'Will you bring us some tea, please, Miss Wilson,' he said to his secretary who was already gliding out of the room. He'd never met Mott, but he'd heard a good deal about him, none of it good. By all accounts the man was a boor and a braggart and a very unpleasant fellow indeed. All the same, his books sold well, there was no denying that; twenty thousand in the hard-cover edition at least, not to mention the paper and serial rights. Hendersons had had a bad time recently, and Mott might be a welcome tonic to their list.

'That's right, do sit down and make yourself comfortable.' He watched Mott throw himself back into the best chair in the room, and leaned gracefully against the mantelpiece. He was about seventy years old, but dressed in the height of juvenile fashion, with wedge-toed shoes, and a wasp-waisted suit that glinted metallically.

'It's a strange coincidence that you should drop in today, Mr Mott. As it happens I've just finished reading your last book, *On the Track of the Snowman*.' The lie came fluently and easily.

'I found it quite fascinating too. Your publishers would be safe in offering a reward for anyone who could put it down unfinished.' Heaven had high hopes as to the purpose of Mott's visit, and he wanted to turn the conversation into the right channels.

'Sales going all right, I trust? Twenty – twenty-five thousand?'

'Twenty-eight to be exact, but it's not all right – not all right at all. Thanks.' Mott scowled and helped himself to one of Heaven's cigarettes.

'Though I say it myself, and I'm the most modest man alive, that book is by far the best thing there's been on the subject, and twenty-eight thousand copies is just chicken-feed. Fifty would have been nearer the mark, in my opinion. When I think of the numbers of books Collins sold about that wretched lion, and compare it to my Snowman – ' He shook his head sadly, and pulled hard on the cigarette.

'Advertising is the real trouble, of course. If that old sheep, Bill Raper, had any sense of proportion he'd have splashed my picture on every magazine and national newspaper in the land. As it is – ' His expression was like that of a spoilt child who feels he has been unfairly denied a treat, and his mind considered the sufferings of other literary figures: Chatterton in his garret, Dean Swift exposed to the jeers of the Dublin mob, Defoe – yes, he was almost certain Defoe had suffered at the hands of some unscrupulous publisher.

'Quite so.' Heaven beamed sympathetically on his guest. The conversation was going just as he hoped.

'A good old firm, Raper and Smith, but rather lacking in vision, perhaps. I would have thought that when they had somebody like yourself on their list – somebody whose books would really sell, given the right treatment – no trouble or expense would be too great.'

'Exactly! They'd sell all right, given decent production and advertising.' Mott had disliked Heaven at first glance, but he really seemed an uncommonly civil and intelligent man when you got to know him.

'I'm quite sure they would, Mr Mott. And if you ever consider a change of publisher, you might keep us in mind. I'm sure you'd find our production satisfactory, and we do try where publicity is concerned. Also we'd be very proud to have you on our list.'

'I bet you would, old boy.' Mott laughed loudly and thumped the arm of his chair. 'Not only proud but overjoyed, I should say. What publisher wouldn't be? Why, if I gave old Raper the brush off, there'd be a queue of you outside my door, cap in hand.

'Yes, I might consider your firm if I ever decided to change, but there's little chance of that, I'm afraid. Raper and Smith have a verbal option on my next two books, and I'm not a man to go back on my word, as you can imagine. Ah, here comes your good lady with our refreshment.' He leered up as Heaven's secretary laid a tray on the desk.

'Yes, so she does. Thank you, Miss Wilson.' There was a marked coldness in Heaven's voice now, for the phrase 'cap in hand' had riled him considerably. Since his hopes of transferring Mott's allegiance had died, he was beginning to regret his hospitality.

'And now, Mr Mott, though I wouldn't describe myself as a busy man, I do have some work to do. Just what is it you wanted to see me about?'

'Oh, yes of course, I was almost forgetting. Cheers!' Mott raised his cup and drank greedily.

'It's an unusual little request, Mr Heaven, but I'd be grateful if you can help. I want to get hold of a book published by the Trefoil Press in 1910. I know it's a hundred to one against, but you might have the blocks or a file copy tucked away somewhere.'

'Published in 1910! That's a very long time ago, and I doubt if – ' For a moment there was merely irritation in Heaven's face, and then his expression altered.

'Mr Mott,' he said, 'just what is the title of this book?'

'It's called *The Grey Boulders*; a volume of mountaineering reminiscences. I say, what's the matter, old boy? Are you feeling all right?'

'Yes, yes, I'm all right. Merely curious.' Heaven moved round to his desk and sat down. In spite of the youthful, glittering suit, he suddenly looked his age.

'Tell me,' he said, 'what is your interest in the book?'

'Oh, quite routine, Mr Heaven. I'm thinking of doing a series of articles on early mountaineering, and *Grey Boulders* would be a pretty handy reference. It seems to be very hard to get hold of, though. That's why I came to you.'

'Yes, it would be difficult to find.' Heaven leaned back in his chair, watching the cigarette smoke drift up to the ceiling.

'I'd just started with the firm when we published that book. Only a hundred copies were printed, and twenty-four of those were destroyed by a fire at our warehouse. The remainder were mostly sold direct to private subscribers. The blocks would have been melted down years ago.

'There was a file copy, though. Yes, until a few months back we did have a copy in file.'

'And it's been stolen or destroyed.' There was no surprise in Mott's voice. Somehow he suspected that this enterprising collector would have paid the publishers a visit. 'Can you tell me what happened?'

'I'll tell you the little I know, Mr Mott, but it is very little.' Heaven's eyes were still fixed on the drifting smoke, and he might have been thinking of all the years he had sat in his office; of dead authors, and forgotten manuscripts, and books which had seemed to be masterpieces and now rotted in damp basements and on six-penny shelves.

'About three months ago, we had a letter from a bookseller asking if we had a copy of *Grey Boulders* available. I can't remember his name, but my secretary might have it.'

'Roach?'

'Yes, that's right, James Roach I think it was. He said he had a customer who wanted it for research, and would pay well for a copy. I wrote back and said that though we obviously had no copy in stock after all these years, we did have a file copy which his customer was welcome to consult on the premises. It's always been the firm's policy to keep a copy of every limited edition we publish, purely for sentimental reasons.

'Anyway, that was the last we heard of Roach, and I presumed he'd found a copy elsewhere. I didn't think any more about him or *Grey Boulders* until our stocktaking six weeks ago.'

'And your file copy had gone?'

'Yes, it had gone all right, and I can't understand it at all. Who would want to steal such a thing?' Heaven shook his head, and his teeth made a sharp, clicking noise.

'Who had the opportunity to steal it, old boy?'

'Well, only Tom Marsden, my clerk, I suppose. The files were kept in a room in the basement, and only he had a key, to the best of my knowledge. If anyone wanted to consult a set of files, they'd ask him for it. But why should old Tom have taken that copy? What possible value could it have been to him? Besides, he'd been with us since he was a boy. I'd have trusted him with my last penny.'

'Perhaps you would, Mr Heaven, but what do we really know about any other human being?' Mott was almost talking to himself, and he imagined how it might have been. Roach's customer had asked him to check with the publishers, and Roach would have written back, saying that though there was no copy for sale, a file copy still existed. It wouldn't have been too difficult to find out who had charge of it.

'Could I speak to this chap Marsden?' he asked.

'Speak to Tom Marsden!' Heaven frowned and shook his head quickly. 'No, that's quite impossible; he's no longer with us, I'm afraid. And though I didn't connect it with Roach's letter or the loss of that book, I wonder – I just wonder – if his death had anything to do with it.'

'You mean – '

'Oh, yes, Mr Mott, I'm afraid so. I was at the inquest, and there was no doubt about it. A few days after I received Roach's letter, old Tom Marsden killed himself.'

★ ★ ★

Two people had died probably because of a book called *Grey Boulders*, and Mr Mott hadn't enjoyed himself so much for years. He swaggered up the steps to the British Museum, and the thought that it might be his duty to talk to the police never occurred to him. Why should it? In his own opinion, his brains and abilities were superior to anything the police could offer, and he also had a personal score to settle. Somehow this killer had discovered that he owned a copy of the book and had broken into his flat to steal it. As far as Mott was concerned, revenge seemed a most worthy motive for tracking him down.

And he could picture exactly what had happened at the publishers. Mr Stanley Heaven might say, 'Old Tom Marsden had been with the firm for years, and I would have trusted him with my last penny,' but the fact remained that old Tom had worked for twelve pounds a week, and had an invalid wife to support. Poor old Tom might not have been averse to accepting a bribe for a small service – the removal of an unimportant book which nobody was likely to miss. And then Tom had died. Yes, that murder had been a very nasty unnecessary crime, with a nasty and thorough mind behind it.

He pushed through the doors into the reading room, checked

his reference, and handed a slip to the attendant. On paper, at least, the Museum had a copy of the book. He just hoped somebody hadn't got to it before him. Then he sat down to wait.

'Nothing but blackamoors seem to use the place these days,' he decided. 'Blackamoors, and Indian students, and Jesuit priests.' He stared scornfully across the vast, circular room with its collection of turbans, clerical collars, and woolly heads bent over learned volumes, and leaned back against the bench. On his right sat two clergymen, one busy reading his office, and the other checking a football coupon.

'Yes, a nasty crime,' he thought. 'Roach's death was quite different, for he had been an unpleasant old man, and probably a blackmailer to boot. But Marsden: no, there'd been no need to kill him.'

He closed his eyes, and considered how it might have started. The first approach, in a pub or café probably, with innocent conversation at the beginning, and then a wheedling voice coming to the point. 'I'm a collector, Mr Marsden, and as you know, we're a crazy lot. All the same, I'd pay well for a small service. Those file copies in your basement, for instance. There's one that's worth fifty pounds to me.' Yes, fifty would be about the figure; not enough to arouse great suspicion, but a very nice sum for a poor man.

Then would come the delivery and payment – Marsden walking down to the Embankment with a parcel under his arm, and nobody about in the midnight streets; the moon shining down on the river, and the sphinxes, and Cleopatra's Needle.

Had Marsden spoken as he handed over that parcel, Mott wondered? Had he looked up, and said, 'You'll never tell anybody will you, sir? I've never been in any trouble before, and – '

But the other voice would have broken in and reassured him. 'Don't worry, Mr Marsden. Don't worry at all. Nobody will ever talk about our transaction; not even you, Mr Marsden.' Then hands and arms would have come up, and Marden's slight body had twisted backwards into the water, while on the Embankment above somebody had walked away, and the sphinxes had gone on smiling.

But *why?* Just what could there be about a book published fifty years ago to provide a motive for two murders? His own blackmail theory was beginning to fade, and he almost accepted John Cain's idea of a mad collector on the rampage.

All the same, *why*? What attraction could there be in the book to drive even a lunatic to murder? Well, in a few minutes he hoped to find out. It would be very difficult, almost impossible, to steal the B.M.'s copy, and from its pages he might begin to learn the truth.

'But *why, why, why*? Just what is there about the bloody book?' Quite involuntarily, but loud and clear, the words burst from his lips and rang across the room like a fog-horn. The cleric at his side frowned, pointed to the 'Silence' notice, and returned to his coupon, glancing coldly at Mott out of the corner of his eye. Some very undesirable people seemed to be allowed to use the reading room these days, he decided.

'The book you asked for, sir.' The attendant had heard Mott's outburst, and even with a whisper he made the 'sir' sound insolent.

'I hope that you'll treat it carefully.'

'Don't worry about that, my man, just put it down and attend to your business.' Mott had noted the insult, and normally he would have given the fellow a piece of his mind. At the moment, however, he was so pleased to find the book intact that he let it pass.

He didn't open it at once, though, but stared down at the cover, almost with love in his eyes. The blue leather had been replaced by a drab library binding, but it was the book he wanted all right. The key which could open the door on a very unpleasant murderer. It might also bring him a good deal of praise, and Mott was fond of praise. Already he seemed to hear the voices of old, authoritative men discussing him in clubs. 'Smart fellow, Moldon Mott.' 'Solved the Clapham and Embankment murders singlehanded.' 'The police thought it was suicide, but once Mott got his nose to the scent, he knew all right.' 'Yes, clever chap, Mott.' 'Mott, Mott, Moldon Mott.' Like a peal of victory his own name rang through his head.

Then at last, slowly and expectantly, a lover approaching the bed of his beloved, an explorer climbing the last pass to an undiscovered country, he lifted the cover and looked at the title page. *The Grey Boulders – An account of British Mountaineering between the years 1840 and 1910.* He picked up the book, turned to the first chapter, and started to read.

And as he did so, every head in the room swung towards him. Black, white, and brown faces took on expressions of shocked astonishment and fury, and three attendants came hurrying across the floor. For Mott's own face had become a mask of baffled fury, and the bellow that burst from his mouth was scarcely human.

'Oh, you bastard,' he shouted at the top of his voice. 'You bloody, wicked, clever bastard!'

All around him the centre pages of the book drifted like confetti, and then turned to anonymous grey powder as they reached the floor.

Eight

'Yes, acid, the devil had used acid.' Mott scowled at John and Julia, and his voice was full of injured dignity as he remembered his humiliation. The pleasure with which he had started to open the book turning to shock and horror as his eyes fell, not on firm pages of print, but grey, rotten pulp that had drifted to powder in his hands. The sequel was hideous, too. With an attendant on either side, and angry or pitying faces staring from each desk, he, Moldon Mott, had been marched into the Curator's office and spoken to as though he were a delinquent schoolboy.

'I see. Rather a neat idea.' In spite of Mott's scowl, John had to grin slightly at the thought, for it was neat. It would have been almost impossible to steal the B.M.'s copy, or even damage it by normal means, so a novel method had been worked out: a little flat capsule of vitriol had been slipped into the centre pages and held there with tape. In time the acid had eaten through the capsule and then started to run through the paper. Though he sympathized with him, there was something very comical in the thought of Mott surrounded by that crumbling confetti, and he was glad to see that Julia felt so too. She was staring intently at the floor and obviously fighting back a smile.

They sat in the office behind his shop, hedged in on every side with piles of unsorted books and unframed prints. Though officially the shop itself was closed, through the glass partition he could see one industrious browser still browsing. He was an old, though not very valued customer, and could be trusted to let himself out.

'Yes, I suppose one could call it neat, in an unpleasant, crazy way.' Mott had obviously noticed Julia's smile and was put out by it.

'We've got a very rum bird on our hands, it seems. When he can buy or steal he does so, when that's impossible he destroys. An

71

efficient blighter, too; he must have got hold of most of the edition by now. But the way, did you know that there were only seventy-six in existence – not a hundred as originally advertised?

'No, well, don't let me teach you your business, but it's a fact. Twenty-four were destroyed in a fire just after binding. Allowing for a normal loss through time, what Roach bought, and what we know to have been destroyed, there can't be many copies about now. My guess is that if we don't get our hands on one of them, we're sunk. Only that book can tell us the kind of man we're up against, and we've got to get hold of a copy – we've got to. I suppose you've had no luck at all, old boy?'

'No, not a smell of the damned book.' John remembered his fruitless hours on the telephone, and the replies which had always been the same. There just didn't seem to be a copy anywhere. 'No, sorry, Cain, but I haven't seen one for years. Why don't you try Francis Edwards?' 'Can't help, old boy. Think I sold a copy some time back, but I can't remember who to. James Thin in Edinburgh might have one.' 'No, sir, we haven't one in stock at the moment. Perhaps the Museum Bookshop in Kendal might help. They carry a very large stock on sporting subjects.'

Yes, always the same: 'Sorry', and advice to try somebody else. 'Try Quaritch, and Maggs, and Commin in Bournemouth, and Hill in Newcastle, and Kerr in Lancashire.' Try anybody you damn well liked, but it didn't do any good. John dreaded the thought of his next phone bill.

'I see. Then we'll just have to hope that our friend panics and shows his hand by attacking you, old boy. Ah, but you've got business to attend to, it seems.' Mott broke off as a knock sounded on the door and the browser came into the office.

'Ah, good evening, Mr Cain.' The man came slowly towards John and he wheezed and creaked like an old gate. He weighed about twenty stone with a great sagging paunch slung in front of him, and grey, mutton-chop whiskers gave him a marked resemblance to the late Emperor Franz Josef of Austria. There was a book in his hand, and he held it out as though it were a rather nasty object and probably laden with germs.

'Sorry to bother you so late, but I found this, and wondered if it is your price-marking. Seems terribly high, you know; thirty shillings!'

'Let me see, Major Allan.' John glanced forward at the book. 'Yes, Ford Madox Ford's *Queen who flew.* I don't think thirty bob is too much. It's a first edition and quite scarce.'

'Yes, yes, but the condition it's in, Mr Cain.' Franz Josef's face looked slightly injured, as though John were an old friend who had let him down badly.

'The spine and covers are rubbed, and there's quite a lot of foxing on the endpapers. Foyle's had one the other day in much better condition for only twenty-five.'

'All right, twenty-five it is then, Major.' Normally John would have used the obvious retort, 'Why didn't you buy Foyle's copy?' and held out for the full amount, but now he just wanted to get rid of the man. He watched him lay the money on the desk and wheeze away, well satisfied with a bargain.

'Humph, big business indeed, old man!' Mott stared scornfully at the money, and then grinned across at Julia. 'Do you manage to make a living out of this dump?'

'Yes, thank you, I make a living.' John suddenly realized that he had rarely disliked a human being as much as he disliked Mott.

It had been very pleasant talking to Julia until a few minutes ago, and then Mott had come shouldering his way into the shop, full of his treatment at the Museum, his discoveries at the publishers', and all the time ogling Julia in a most horrible way. 'My dear Miss Lent, what a great pleasure it is to meet you – I do hope our young friend Cain hasn't been boring you – Oh, your uncle has had another stroke, then! I am so very sorry. Wonderful man he must be; one of the last great captains of industry still left. Please accept my wishes for a speedy recovery.' Yes, John was beginning to loathe Mr Mott.

The worst of it was that Julia had seemed to appreciate Mott. She had blushed at his compliments, appeared grateful for his sympathy, and listened with rapt attention to the boastful account of his doings.

Yes, damn Julia too, he thought. He had as much chance of even dating her, as of finding an original papyrus of the Book of Genesis. Girls like Julia Lent didn't even notice little second hand dealers in suburban back-streets. All at once he wanted to be done with the whole affair.

'And my business is no concern of anyone,' he said coldly, 'except in so far as it concerns one book. A book which has probably killed two people already. We can't get hold of a copy, so don't you both think it's about time we all went to the police and told them what we know? They'd have to act on what the three of us could tell them.'

'No, I damn well don't think so.' Mott flushed angrily. 'On the whole the police are industrious but unimaginative men. What can they discover that – that – ' He was about to say 'I', but gallantly changed it to, 'that Miss Lent and ourselves are unable to.' He beamed on Julia as though she were a clever child.

'And now, my dear, though I know how upset you must be by Sir Stephen's illness, you must try and help me. Was there anyone in your house, a relative, a servant, a visitor, who might have taken the book and had a connection with the Metropolitan Library?'

'No, nobody that I know of.' Julia shook her head quickly. 'You see, it might have been stolen months ago, and almost anybody could have taken it. My uncle is a member of the Metropolitan, I think, but I don't believe he's been there for years. I couldn't ask him any questions, of course. The doctor said it may be days before he's allowed to talk.'

She looked away from Mott and John, and suddenly she felt very guilty. The three of them were partners in a sense, and she had no right to hold back information. All the same, she had to. She had told them some of the truth, but not all of it. She couldn't do that. She could say that her uncle had had a stroke, but not how it came to him. Not how his face had looked when she told him of John's theory, or how his voice had sounded as he fell towards Peter Trew. 'Just a lunatic – oh, Julie, my dear, if only he were right!' She had no idea what the book might contain, but she was quite certain of one thing: it terrified her uncle, and was somehow connected with the Lent family.

'Another customer, old boy? More big business?' Mott's voice broke into her thoughts, as a light tapping sounded on the outer door.

'No, not a customer, my assistant, I think. I sent her round to Roach's house to see if there was any afternoon mail.' John got up and walked out through the shop. Sure enough, the girl was waiting at the door with a thin bundle of letters in her hand. He thanked her and wished her good night, watching her walk away past a big car that was parked a little way down the street. A foolish place to leave it, he thought, for the street was very narrow there. If its owner wasn't lucky, he'd find a police ticket on the windscreen when he got back.

At first glance Roach's mail was quite unimportant; a sale catalogue, the final notice of the gas bill, and a letter from a Chicago dealer wanting books on early fire-arms. He pushed them to one side, and picked up the last envelope. It was thick and creamy, and addressed in a very beautiful hand, as though by someone who regarded penmanship as much an art as a means of communication. Quite idly he tore the flap and pulled out a single sheet of notepaper with a nicely printed address: 'Pear Tree Cottage, Evelyn Village, Hertfordshire.'

'Dear Mr Roach,' he read. 'It must be almost a year since we met, but I hope you haven't forgotten our little transaction.

'If not, you may remember asking me to contact you, should I wish to dispose of any more of my cousin's books, and in particular of the second copy of – '

'Yes, yes indeed! I think we've got a break at last.' John whistled with surprise, but before he could go on, Mott reached out and grabbed the letter from him. For a moment he squinted at it, and then a great, wide grin opened up his face.

'Yes, we've got a break all right. Listen to this, my dear.' He leaned forward into the light and read aloud to Julia.

' " – the second copy of a book entitled *Grey Boulders*, which I told you had been mislaid. As it happens this has now materialized, and should you wish to purchase it, I would be glad if you would call and see me. As I am completely confined to the house now, there is no need for you to bother to make an appointment. Yours very truly – Gwendoline Bell."

'Yes, we're on the way home at last.' A roar of triumph broke from Mott's lips, and he smote John hard and painfully across the shoulder.

'Yes, Hallelujah, here I come!' He hurled back his chair, and broke into a grotesque jig of delight, holding the letter like a dancing partner in his great, ape-like arms, and singing as he did so.

'Gwen-do-line Bell, Dilly Dilly, Gwendoline Bell.' He crooned loudly and tunelessly, waltzing across the room and knocking over a pile of books that barred his way.

'Lavender's blue, Dilly Dilly, Gwendoline's swell. Oh how I love you, Miss Gwendoline Bell.' He lifted the letter to his lips and gave it a smacking kiss.

'Yes, we're in luck, my dears. Now we have something to get our teeth into at last.' He came to rest by the table, beaming down at them.

'Let's see, though. Evelyn's a good hour's run from here, so we'd better get cracking right away. From her tone I imagine Gwendoline is an elderly maiden lady and a stickler for the proprieties. It won't do to arrive late, or for all of us to go barging in. Now which of us shall go? Yes, fair's fair, and I'll toss you for it, Cain.' He pulled a shilling out of his pocket and flicked it on to his palm.

'You call, will you? Heads, eh? And tails it is.' Before John could even glance at the coin he had tucked it away, and started to tighten his coat.

'Well, I'll be on my way. Get in touch with you as soon as I'm back. And once again, it's been a great pleasure to meet you, my dear.' To John's disgust he bent down and kissed Julia's hand before hurrying purposefully to the door.

★ ★ ★

'You really loathe him, don't you?' Julia got up from her chair and smiled at John. 'You'd like to cut him into little pieces and – '

'And flush him down the drain. Yes, I most certainly would.'

She had so completely echoed his thoughts that in spite of himself John had to smile back.

'I don't know anybody who's got on my nerves as much as Mott. If I wasn't sure that he could tear me apart with one hand, I'd give him a punch on his horrible nose.'

'Yes, I'm sure you would; poor John.' Her sleeve brushed against his arm as she moved to the door, and he smelt a faint trace of some very expensive perfume.

'Yes, Mott's a very trying individual, and I'm quite sure he cheated with that coin. All the same I'm glad he's gone to Evelyn and left us alone for a bit. You see, I'd like you to buy me a drink.'

'And I'd like to do that very much.' He paused and grinned at her. 'That is, if you think I can afford to.'

'What! Oh, I see. Mott's comment on making a living still rankles, does it?' She looked around the shelves as she spoke.

'I'd say you can afford it all right. You seem to have quite a good stock at the moment.'

'Thanks. You know anything about the second-hand book trade?'

'Yes, as a matter of fact I worked in a shop once. You may know it, "Reason's Corner", in Swiss Cottage. An aunt of mine owned it.'

'I know it all right.' John's grin widened as he remembered a mock Tudor frontage with rows of forbidding titles in the windows, and a coffee bar at the back. On the surface a beatnik haunt, but with a difference. Whatever their appearance, its customers had well-filled wallets and cheque books stuffed into their jeans.

'Did your aunt run it for profit, or merely as a hobby?'

'Oh, she made a profit all right. Our family always seem to make a profit. She had rather a good gimmick, as it happens – perhaps the best gimmick there is where the British public is concerned. She was against things.'

'Against things? What sort of things?'

'Oh, things that people disapprove of; blood sports, and the colour bar, bishops and the H-bomb, capital punishment and the House of Lords. Her shop was always full of well-meaning loonies and she made a very good thing out of it. Thanks.' Julia moved forward as he held open the door for her, and looked at the side window. Its lower half was almost filled by a Hogarth folio, open at the centre plate of the Harlot's Progress.

'That poor girl's been in your window too long,' she said. 'The page is curling and she's getting a little fly-blown.'

'I know it. I'll change her in the morning.' John shut the door and locked the mortise.

'As it happens, I had a note shoved through the door about her the other day. It said – "Dear Sir, Could you please turn a page so that we can see the Harlot progress a little farther."

'And now let's progress towards that drink, there's a pub just a few minutes down the road.' He took her arm and they began to walk forward through the dusk. As they did so, the engine of the parked car started.

John's shop was almost at the end of a row, and after it the street narrowed, and became flanked by park railing on one side and a churchyard wall on the other; a very unimportant street which was usually deserted at this time of evening. They were perhaps twenty yards along the wall when they heard the car.

It could only have taken seconds, but it seemed like a year. One moment they were just two ordinary people on their way to a drink, and the next they were running. One moment the car was just an ordinary mass-produced saloon, purring slowly down the road with its side-lights gleaming through the slight fog, and the next it was a weapon, a crazed monster leaping up over the pavement with the headlamps bearing down on them like a target, and the wheels pointing straight at them.

And there was not a single thing they could do about it. No doorway to run into, no lamp-post to dodge behind, nothing at all. John hurled Julia against the wall and covered her with his body, but he knew it was useless. Mott's warning was very loud in his head against the roar of the engine. 'We can safely expect an attack on your life during the next twenty-four hours.' He loathed Mott, but the man's prophecy was coming true. The person who had killed Roach and Marsden was going to kill again, and there was nothing to be done about it. They clung to each other like lovers, and waited for death.

Then suddenly it happened. The bumpers were within feet of crushing them against the wall, when the roar of the engine changed to screaming brakes, and the wheels swung out and clawed sideways and away from them. John felt no spine-crushing blow, but a light slap on the buttocks as the rear mudguard struck him, and then the car accelerated again, and tore away out of sight. Either a miracle had taken place, or this eccentric killer had lost his nerve or had a change of heart.

For a long time they leaned against that wall, still clinging to each other, and thanking whatever fate had saved them. Then they inspected the damage. It was very slight. Just a long tear across the seat of John's trousers, and not nearly enough to stop them enjoying the drink they had both wanted, and now really needed.

Nine

EVELYN was still a small, unspoilt village, and it didn't take Mott long to find Pear Tree Cottage. It stood at the end of a narrow lane, and was very 'Olde Worlde', but in the best sense of the term, with genuine Jacobean chimneys and local tile. He climbed out of the car, noting a 'No Hawkers' sign on the gate, and grinned at an arrow below it which pointed to the Tradesmen's Entrance. On his present errand, he supposed that he might be regarded as a tradesman, and the thought that anybody would suggest that he used the back door amused him a good deal. He marched up the garden path, and gave the front-door bell a long peal.

'Good evening, sir.' The maid who answered the door seemed to have come from another century with a frilly apron, celluloid cuffs, and ribbons in her cap. She looked about as old as the house.

'Good evening, my dear. I have called to see Miss Gwendoline Bell. My name is Mott – J. Moldon Mott.' He paused to allow this important piece of information to sink in, then, as her face remained blank, reluctantly added, 'Would you tell her it concerns a Mr James Roach.'

'Oh, I see, sir. Yes, I think we've been expecting a visit from Mr Roach. Would you wait a minute, please, and I'll just tell the mistress you're here.' She hurried away with a loud rustling of starched linen, but was back within seconds.

'Please come this way, sir. Miss Bell will see you at once.'

The room smelt of lavender and wax polish, and was lit by a single standard lamp. A woman was sitting under the lamp, and she put aside a piece of embroidery she had been working on as Mott came through the doorway. She was dressed in black, and though obviously very old, sat in her straight chair as stiff as a ramrod.

'Good evening, sir. Please excuse my not getting up, but I'm under doctor's orders. I'm so sorry Mr Roach was unable to come himself. I do hope he is quite well.'

'Yes, he's well enough, Madam.' Mott didn't really like lying, but it seemed necessary. This old battle-axe obviously wished to deal with Roach, and might turn difficult if she heard he no longer existed.

'I'm a friend of his, and as I had to be in the vicinity today, he asked me to call and pick up a book from you. I have your letter to him here.'

'Thank you.' She glanced at the note, and then looked at Mott. As she did so her polite smile died, and was replaced by an expression of keen curiosity. Though Mott had the hide of a rhinoceros, he felt a slight twinge of embarrassment under those piercing eyes.

'But don't I know you?' she said. 'Haven't we met somewhere before? Yes, your face is very familiar. Let me see – Knott, Roland Knott? Oh, of course, how very stupid of me.' Like a backcloth parting the smile returned to her face, but there was more than conventional politeness in it now. It was delighted surprise, and excitement, and hero-worship rolled into one.

'You're Mr Mott, aren't you – *the* Moldon Mott – the author of all those wonderful books. Poor Ethel, my maid, is getting very deaf, I'm afraid, and must have mis-heard your name. Oh, this is a pleasure, Mr Mott. Please do sit down.'

'Thank you, Miss Bell.' There was an unctuous smirk on Mott's face as he lowered his bulk on to a frail Jacobean chair.

'Do I detect a fan?' he said gallantly.

'A fan! But that's an understatement if ever there was one. I don't know anything that gives me as much pleasure as your books. Not only exciting, but so well written and scholarly, too. I read them at a sitting when they come out, and then pick them up and read them over and over again. Look!' With the air of Puss in Boots presenting his own riches to the Marquis of Carabas, she tilted the lamp, and a line of Mott's gaudy volumes glinted back at him. He decided that Miss Bell wasn't a battle-axe at all, but a most charming and intelligent woman.

'And, as you are here, I wonder if you would do something terribly kind for me, Mr Mott?' she said. 'I know how a man like yourself must be bothered by your public, but it would give me so much pleasure if you would – '

'If I would sign them for you, eh? But of course, dear lady.' Mott pulled out a pen and bounded to the shelf. He bore what he imagined to be the expression of the lost heir suddenly revealed – the exiled prince returned to his adoring subjects. In reality it was much closer to the grin of an intelligent ape, rewarded with a banana after joining two sticks together.

'Now, let me see. What shall I write? Yes, "To Miss Gwendoline Bell in friendship and respect". How's that?' He signed with a flourish, and turned to the next volume.

'Oh, that is kind of you, Mr Mott!' She looked at the inscription as though it were a cheque for a million pounds.

'And won't my friends be excited! You have several admirers in the village, you know, and when they see this – '

'They'll be green with envy, I expect.' Mott had finished his pleasant task now, and beamed down at her.

'They most certainly will. The vicar's wife – rather a boastful woman, I'm sorry to say – has two books signed by Sir Philip Gibbs, but this will put her nose out of joint.

'Oh, but I'm so sorry, Mr Mott. Here am I chattering away, and quite forgetting my duties as a hostess. Would you care for a glass of sherry? There should be a decanter on the sideboard over there.'

'Thank you, a glass of sherry would be most pleasant.' Mott poured out two generous measures. As a rule he disliked sherry, but this time it seemed to go down very well. Miss Bell really was a pleasant woman. He pulled up a chair beside her, and for a time quite forgot his reason for calling as they fell to discussing the three topics which interested him most in life; himself, his exploits, and the fate which usually befell his detractors.

'Oh, yes, I've known fear, dear lady, but somehow I've always managed to put it behind me. Once up the Amazon, for instance . . . The brute weighed over a ton and a half, and was coming for us at twenty miles an hour . . . I got the blighter by the seat of his pants and threw him over the side on to the dock – '

Yes, Mott really enjoyed himself, and so did Miss Bell, for she

thought Mott a fine man; far, far superior in real life to her wildest imaginings. A proper man, of a type that had seemed to die
out when she was a girl and leave nothing but weaklings behind.
Her early reading had been confined to the hero cult as typified by
Messrs Henty, Scott, and Rider Haggard, and Mott seemed to fill
all these authors' requirements with credit. It was after ten, and
a grim-faced Ethel had informed her mistress that bed-time was
long overdue, when at last they got down to business.

'But of course, the book which you called to collect, Mr Mott.
I have it here all ready for you. I suppose you are a client of Mr
Roach's, rather than a personal friend? Yes, I fancied that was the
case, though, for a dealer, he seemed quite a well educated man.

'No, no, I'd much rather not discuss money with you. Just ask
Roach to send me a cheque for what he thinks it's worth.'

'Thank you, Miss Bell. Thank you very much indeed.' There
was a wide smile of triumph on his face as Mott took the book
from her, for he felt that he had gone a step forward at last. A little
octavo volume, with its pale-blue binding shining like silk in his
hand. He flicked it open and his smile widened. There was no acid
here, and no mutilation. This was a perfect copy, the real McCoy
which might tell him what he wanted to know.

'But this is quite a rare book, Miss Bell,' he said at last. 'How did
you manage to come by two copies?'

'Oh, didn't Roach tell you? They belonged to my cousin, David
Blythe. He was responsible for some of the illustrations, and when
the book came out he put his name down for a copy, though the
publishers gave him a complimentary one as well. Rather a con-
ceited man, I'm afraid.

'Yes, poor David. We were never very close, and it came as a
great surprise when he wrote and asked if I would store some of
his books for him. It seemed that he had moved into a smaller
house, and had very little room. When he died last year, I felt I
had the right to dispose of the books as I felt fit. A friend gave me
Roach's name as a possible purchaser, and I wrote to him.

'Yes, poor old David.' She shook her head slowly. 'I think those
books were probably the only things he ever loved.'

'And he was responsible for some of the illustrations, was he?' Mott turned to the first plate; a photograph of the Tower Ridge on Ben Nevis, and the credit beneath it read, 'The Rev. David Blythe – Glencarron Rectory, Inverness-shire.' A tiny spasm of fear ran through his mind as he looked at it, and he remembered how Roach and the publishers' clerk had died. The killer could easily have found that this nice woman possessed copies of the book, and he hated the thought of anything happening to her.

'Why do you keep saying *poor* David, Miss Bell?'

'Because he was poor, Mr Mott. Poor, and lonely, and very embittered. He got the living of Glencarron when he was a young man, but he never got anything else. There was something rather unattractive about his personality, I think, and his church was always empty. He applied for other livings, but the bishops always passed him over.

'Also he never had the recognition he felt he deserved as a photographer and naturalist, and that soured him. From what I've heard, he must have been a very sad and rather nasty old man at the end.'

'Nasty?' Mott raised his eyebrows.

'Yes, very nasty, I'm afraid. Mean and vicious and cruel, too.' She frowned slightly, as though concentrating.

'I'll try to explain what I mean. If one steals for gain, for instance, it's very reprehensible, but perhaps not wicked. If on the other hand one steals purely for pleasure – for the joy of depriving somebody of something they were fond of, then I think that is wicked. David never stole, of course, but he seems to have been that kind of person. The Germans have a word for it which can't really be translated into English – *Schadenfreude*.'

'Yes, I know it, "Joy caused by another person's despair". That is unpleasant.' Mott had a picture of the Reverend David Blythe now, and a theory was starting to form in his head.

'It is, isn't it? And I'm afraid quite true, Mr Mott. There were so many horrible stories told about him. At the end he was almost attacked by the villagers, and the bishop had to force him to retire.

'But I must be boring you, Mr Mott, and in any case I shouldn't speak evil of the dead. Poor David is much better forgotten.'

'You're not boring me, Miss Bell. You couldn't bore me if you tried.' Mott bowed gallantly. 'But this second copy of the book that he sent you: I understand it was lost for a time?'

'That's right. It just seemed to vanish, and I couldn't think what had happened. Then last week it turned up again, behind the bookcase. It must have slipped down and got wedged there. My poor Ethel is very old, and becoming rather careless about dusting, I'm afraid. Really a most badly educated woman, too.' Miss Bell flushed with annoyance. 'I can't tell you how humiliated I feel that she announced you so wrongly. Oh, there you are, Ethel!' Her face dropped as the woman appeared in the doorway with a hot-water bottle in her hand and a scowl on her face.

'Yes, I know it's bed-time, Ethel, and I'm coming now, my dear.' She pulled herself painfully up from the chair.

'No, it may be a cold night, but I intend to show our guest out myself. Though you didn't realize it, he happens to be a very important man indeed.'

She took Mott's arm and walked very stiffly to the front door. There was a great glow of pleasure in her eyes as he promised to call and see her again, kissed her hand, and then bounded boyishly down the path.

Ten

'BUT there isn't anything to be learned from the blasted book; there isn't a single damn thing.' Backwards and forwards, deep in thought, between the skull lamps and the devil masks, Mott paced the floor of his den.

'No, there's nothing there – nothing at all.' He flung the book down on his desk in disgust, and pulled back the curtains. Outside it was full morning. He had spent over eight hours going through that copy of *Grey Boulders*, studying every page and illustration for a clue, but he wasn't an inch farther forward.

Not that he had had any firm idea of what he was looking for, of course; some suggestion of a forgotten crime committed a long time ago, perhaps; some hint of a family skeleton hidden in its pages which could drive an unbalanced mind to murder.

But he was wrong it seemed, and John Cain was right. The nigger in this wood-pile was just some crazy collector who hoarded copies of the book like a magpie, and destroyed those he couldn't buy or steal; a very dull solution indeed. He'd like the idea of that long-forgotten family skeleton being brought to light.

All the same, now that they had a copy of the book, there was an easy way of bringing this maniac into the open. Let Cain put it up for public auction with a big, thumping reserve on the price, and wait to see who bought it. Contemptible, really, like shooting a sitting bird, but probably the only sensible course. He stared gloomily out over the park, feeling bitter disappointment, and thinking how much he would have enjoyed a really splendid dénouement. Then he turned back to his desk as the phone rang.

'Oh, it's you, old boy,' he said, as he heard John's voice. 'Yes, I got the book all right, but it's not much use to us, I'm afraid – not so far anyway.

'What's that you say? Yes, I see – I really do see.' As he listened to John's account of the night before, and the car which had so miraculously turned aside, his face altered. All the tiredness left it, and it became heavy and thoughtful, with a little ticking pulse in the forehead.

'No, old boy,' he said. 'No, I don't think it was just a drunk who lost control of his car for a second. It was your executioner all right, and he didn't have a change of heart at the last moment or lose his nerve. If my hunch is right, something quite different stopped him.

'By the way, are you alone at the moment? Good. Then listen to me. I may be libelling a perfectly respectable group of people, but there's a way of making sure. I want you to have the book put up for auction, but it mustn't go into the sale rooms until the very last moment. We can't risk our friends getting hold of it there. Unless my arithmetic is at fault, this is probably one of the very few copies still in existence. Can you manage that?

'Good. No, I'm not going to tell you what I think yet, as I may be hideously wrong. I'll check first, and then I'll call you back.

'And Cain! If you're at all fond of little Miss Julia, just pray that I am wrong.'

He replaced the phone, and then reached out across the desk and pulled the book towards him. He'd got a firm theory at last, and in a few moments he might be able to prove it. That speeding car which had turned aside had given him the key he wanted. All the same, how he hoped he was wrong.

Very slowly he turned the pages till the book lay open at a plate in its centre, and in his mind's eye he could imagine another man looking at that photograph. The man would have looked quite idly at first, just browsing along, with no particular interest because he had seen the picture a score of times before. And then, quite suddenly, he might have noticed a little, tiny detail, and felt his world go crashing down.

Yes, Mott could almost see how the man's face would have looked as he bent over a magnifying glass and knew the truth. Fifty years ago his family had numbered a murderer amongst its members, and if that fact ever became public, it would spell ruin. Fifty years was a long time, but the descendant of a murderer cannot profit from his crime. Yes, that man could have had a very good reason for destroying those books, just as the driver of the car had good reason to pull aside when he saw not merely John Cain and an unknown woman in his lights, but Julia Lent.

He looked at the caption beneath the illustration. 'October the sixteenth, 1909,' he read. 'The last climb of the Lent Brothers. A few moments after this picture was taken by the Reverend David Blythe, Hal Lent fell from the Great Flake on Ben Gael, and met his death; the end of a very great climber.'

'But did he really fall, or was he pulled? Did his brother pull him?' Mott muttered the words aloud as he bent over the photograph. It had been taken from a distance, and the face of the cliff, which at close range would appear as a mass of broken cracks and ridges, stood out like a smooth wall. Far beyond its shoulder could be seen the huge pyramid of the Bald Mountain with a plume of cloud on its summit, and, in the centre of the picture, two tiny dots which were the climbers.

Mott had very few nerves, but his hand shook slightly with excitement as he held a magnifying glass above those dots, and they swam into focus. Two men climbing a mountain a long time ago – two men tied together by a rope, scrambling up over the Flake of Ben Gael. And then one of those men had fallen, and the rope between them had snapped, and he had gone spinning down to the screes three hundred feet below.

But if he hadn't fallen – if Hal Lent hadn't slipped or misjudged the distance – if he had been pulled backwards by a rope held by his brother, which broke because it was three-quarters cut through – if the photograph showed that, then there was a very good reason for somebody to destroy the books that contained it.

'Damnation!' Mott hadn't really wanted his theory to be true, but his face contorted with baffled fury, and the glass flew from his hand to shatter against the wall. For he was wrong, it seemed – pathetically wrong. The enlarged picture showed no sign of murder, but just two men climbing a mountain together; two men who knew their skill perfectly.

Hal Lent stood on a little ledge reaching up for a handhold, and the rope hanging from his waist was slack and comfortable. Forty feet below, his brother leaned back against the cliff face, tied to a pillar of rock as a belay, and he wasn't even looking up at Hal, but was staring out across the valley with a pipe between his teeth. The Lent family were in the clear, it seemed.

All the same, there was something strange. Mott crossed to his bookcase and pulled out a volume of the *Scottish Mountaineering Club Guide.* Yes, here it was:

> The Great Flake on Ben Gael. This climb is five hundred and twenty feet long, and requires seventy feet of rope between the climbers. The start begins almost at the centre of the main scree slope, and one proceeds straight up a broken ridge for two hundred and fifty feet till a chimney is reached –

Mott turned a page, and glanced at a beautifully sketched diagram of the mountain. He read on,

> The climb is not popular today, partly because Ben Gael has no other route of interest to attract visitors, and partly because the rock is loose and rotten in places. By modern standards the exposure and technical problems are slight, though a swinging chockstone at the end of the fourth pitch presents some difficulty. It was at this point that a fatal accident occurred in –

'The technical problems are slight!' Then why – why should Hal Lent, one of the finest climbers of his day, have fallen? Even though the accident took place in October with early snow on the hills, even though the rock was loose and rotten, a mountaineer of that calibre shouldn't have fallen. He picked up the copy of *Grey Boulders* and looked at William Lent's account of the accident.

> My brother must have been approaching the top of the second chimney when he fell. I did not see the accident myself, being screened by the corner of the buttress, and the

rope between us was at an angle of about sixty degrees. As soon as I heard him call out and start to fall, I pulled in the rope, but it caught over a jagged ridge of rock and broke.

I have no idea at all why my brother should have fallen. He was a most experienced climber, and quite familiar with the route, which is not unduly difficult. The only explanation I can offer is that, when he was negotiating the swinging chockstone in the chimney, something occurred to distract his attention.

So much for Brother William, but though he was obviously in the clear as far as murder was concerned, Mott wanted to know more about that climb. A lot of weather would have blown across those hills in fifty years, but he wondered if the broken face of Ben Gael might not still tell him something. He also wanted to know much more about the man who had taken that photograph.

Thought was action where Mott was concerned, and almost at once he got to work. His first job was to make two telephone calls, one to John, and the other to the agreeable Miss Bell. As soon as he had finished he wrenched open a cupboard and started to collect his climbing kit.

* * *

'No, no, no, Mr Cain, most certainly not.' Gordon Angel, manager of the Compton Gallery and Sale Rooms, frowned and gracefully lowered his rump against what had been described to him as a genuine Sheraton writing-table. It creaked loudly in protest, but he wouldn't have cared if it had fallen to pieces. Whatever its owner might say, one glance at the grain had told him it was sham, and pretty poor sham too. He would see that it was returned that very afternoon. The Compton was not a place to suffer junk gladly.

'No, it's quite out of the question, I'm afraid – quite impossible.' He wore a completely black suit relieved by a dove-grey tie, and an air of immense dignity. The kind of man one associated with Masonic functions, and after-dinner speeches of interminable length, and heavy platitudes directed against the younger generation. The kind of man one would love to see sit on a tack.

'And you should know us well enough by now, Mr Cain, to be sure we'd help if we could. Yes, if it were merely a question of holding back a cheque for a few days, or arranging for a private view, the Compton would help out; always ready to assist a good friend or a valued client.

'But this! Most certainly not. And I'm surprised that you should ask such a thing, Mr Cain. A young man like yourself, on the threshold of his career – our duty to the trade and the public to consider – a reputation built up by over fifty years of straight dealing – ' Like a river in flood the platitudes rolled grandly out.

'But you have my word that the book is all right.' John fought back irritation, for he realized Angel's difficulty. He and Mott had decided that the book must be kept in a bank till the day of the sale, and it was asking a bit much for him to advertise it without seeing it. All the same, Angel was a pompous ass, and it would do no harm to deflate his dignity. Tucked away in John's mind was a certain piece of information which could show Mr Gordon Angel in a very poor light if it were made public. He didn't want to use it, but the threat was there if necessary.

'Yes, yes, your word, Mr Cain, and a very good word too, as I know well. All the same you must consider it from our point of view.' If an elephant could speak John was sure it would be in just such a pompous, pedantic manner.

'My brother-in-law, a licensed victualler, I'm sorry to say, and rather a common sort of man, informs me that he has similar problems. He would like to cash cheques for his more favoured customers, but if he did so, all the rag, tag, and bobtail in the bar would try to follow suit.' Angel had only a nose, not a trunk, to swing, but he shook his head as though he imagined this were the case.

'Besides, what you're asking me to do is hardly ethical, and the Compton couldn't get mixed up in anything like that, could it, now?'

'No, I suppose not.' John started slightly as a car backfired in the street, and Mott's warning that the killer would strike again was very close. Everyone who spoke to him, every sudden movement or noise, seemed like a threat, and his nerves were like raw wounds. He had carried out Mott's instructions to the letter, not even discussing them with Julia, though he'd wanted to do that very much, and the trap was almost sprung. Only this pompous elephant – no, not an elephant, they have a sense of humour – this hippopotamus of a man held him back.

'Of course not, my dear fellow. Why, in almost fifty years of business the Compton has never been mixed up in anything underhand or shady.' A still louder creak came from the table, and Angel eased himself to his feet. He didn't mind breaking the so-called Sheraton, but a fall would be a severe blow to his dignity. Besides, he wanted to show this persistent young man that his time was up. He pulled a gleaming full-hunter watch from his pocket and glanced meaningfully at it.

'Yes, just think what you're asking us to do, Cain. To advertise a book in our next catalogue, without even checking or collating it – without even seeing it, or putting it on view. No, quite out of the question.'

'But I promise you, Mr Angel, that the book is in mint condition, and will be delivered to you in good time for the sale.' John was rapidly coming to the end of his tether. The man really was a hippo; a great, smug, self-satisfied hippo wallowing contentedly in some muddy backwater. Well, the hippo was in for a severe shock if he didn't learn manners.

'Oh, I'm quite sure it would be, Cain, but my answer is still No.' He lowered his voice slightly.

'Besides, there's something fishy about those copies of Grey Boulders, I think. Something I don't want to be mixed up with. Oh yes, one may have fetched an absurd price the other day, because of a feud between Roach and Lehman, but I wonder.

'And the reserve you're asking me to put on it. A hundred pounds! No, no offence, Mr Cain, but something smells a little, and we at the Compton Gallery have our reputations to think of. No offence to you personally of course.' As though proving there was no offence, he raised a great, flabby hand in an attitude of benediction.

'No, you're obviously just the agent for some eccentric customer, I think. Why don't you try Hudson's or Sommerlee's, if you must go through with your scheme? They might help, though personally I doubt it.'

'I might have to do that, Mr Angel. I came to you first, because I thought we were friends. After the Countess of Bristol's sale, for instance – ' John's voice hardened.

'The Bristol sale!' The hippo had looked up from the water now, and there was a twinge of anxiety in its little pig-like eyes.

'That's right; the collection of nautical books you sold last year. Surely you haven't forgotten, Mr Angel.' John disliked Mott intensely, but he suddenly pictured himself in a Mottish role, crawling through the jungle with a sun helmet well down and his rifle pointing at the hippo's thick hide.

'I bought one lot, you remember. *The Domain of Neptune*, that eighteenth-century manual of seamanship. You rather decried it at the sale because it was imperfect. I remember you holding it up, and saying it was a pity that such a good book appeared to have been scribbled on by a mischievous child.'

'Did I? Well, well, that's all past history, isn't it?' The hippo had scented the hunter now, and couldn't make up its mind whether to charge or beat a hasty retreat.

'And you made a good profit, Mr Cain. A very good profit, so let's forget about it. Everybody makes the odd mistake from time to time.'

'Yes, of course they do. All the same, it's a lucky thing I had a private customer for that book, isn't it? Otherwise I'd have had to advertise it to the trade, and the full story would have come out.' John's hand was on the trigger now, and tightening for first pressure.

'I wonder what would have happened to your reputation if people knew what those marginal scribbles you decried really were. I wonder what the Countess of Bristol would say if she knew what my customer paid for that book. Oh, yes, I promised to keep quiet, Mr Angel, but you also promised that if ever I needed a favour in return – '

'All right, Cain, you win.' The hippo had decided that discretion was the better part of valour, and dived to the muddy depths of its pool. Angel pulled out a pad and a gold-topped pen.

'We'll put your book as the last lot of the day, then. Yes, One copy *Grey Boulders*, Trefoil Press Limited Edition – ' His hand shook slightly as he wrote, for the mention of that sailing manual had given him a bad turn.

Well it might. Both his own dignity and the Gallery's reputation would suffer a severe jolt if the full story became public. His evaluation of the book had been made after a single quick glance, while John's came from a hunch, followed by several hours' work in the library of the Imperial War Museum. The marginal scribbles he had decried had indeed been written by a child. His name happened to be Mr Midshipman Horatio Nelson.

Eleven

'AYE, Mr Mott, a fearful man was the Reverend David Blythe.'

Mrs Annie McDoggart, landlady of the Glencarron Arms Hotel, hadn't liked the look of her guest from the start, and with the passage of time dislike had grown to cold fury. For this Mr Mott had seemed to imagine that the hotel was his private property, and she his servant. He had complained that the room was too small and the bed damp, decried her cooking, rung for whisky at midnight, and generally made a thorough nuisance of himself. Only during the last thirty minutes had her opinion begun to be modified, for there was no denying that he was a good listener, and she loved to gossip. Almost all the local scandal seemed to interest him.

'Aye, a bad man, and we're well rid of him.' Once again she recounted the late rector's sins: acts of uncharity and meanness, cruelty to children and animals, failure to visit the dying, and refusal to conduct weddings unless both parties had been regular attenders at his church.

'A bad man, sir, and a bad end.'

'Yes, you were going to tell me about his end.' Mott pushed aside the remains of his breakfast and lit a cigarette. With his oilskin jacket, enormous nailed boots, and great gingery thighs bursting out of leather shorts, he presented a sinister or comical figure, depending on the viewer's temperament.

'He was burnt in his bed, wasn't he?'

'That he was, sir. Just over a year ago, it must have been. He'd moved up the Glen a few months before. The bishop had had to take action, you see, after that business of Mary Duncan.'

'Mary Duncan?'

'Aye, poor old Mary. She was Blythe's housekeeper, and he turned her out after thirty years' service, and her with nowhere in the world to go. Said the poor soul was too old for her work and he had no more use for her. Some of the lads were for going up to the rectory and tarring and feathering him for that.' There was a wistful look in Mrs McDoggart's eyes, and she obviously wished they had done so.

'Anyhow, the laird, Sir Archibald Bethune, stepped in. Went over to see the bishop, and said there'd be sore trouble in the village unless the rector was moved. The bishop acted double quick then. Blythe was made to retire, and bought a little croft up the glen. You can see it from the window, sir. Just under the shoulder of the hill.'

'Yes, so I can.' Mott squinted up the valley. Where the stream turned away to the south, he could just make out the shell of a ruined cottage.

'A lonely place. Did he live there by himself?'

'That he did, sir. Nobody would have much to do with him, after the way he'd treated Mary Duncan. Excepting Dr MacBain, that is; very charitable man, the doctor. He'd ride over now and again and see how Blythe was. Said there was some good in all of us, if only you'd look for it.'

'Did he indeed? How very foolish of him.' Mott was a strong believer in original sin, if not in original virtue.

'Is this doctor still alive?'

'Indeed he is, sir. A wonderful old man, the doctor. I saw him go off early this morning on his pony; probably on his way to Sheil Water for some fishing. That's on the other side of Ben Gael. He's nearly eighty, and his son runs the practice now, but he still rides all over these hills. They don't build them like that these days, sir.'

'Don't they, indeed.' Mott found the remark extremely distasteful. In his own opinion no generation had produced a finer physical specimen than himself.

'And this fire? How did it happen?'

'Well, nobody rightly knows, Mr Mott. Everything was destroyed before the brigade got there, you see. All the same it seems probable that he knocked over an oil lamp; terribly dangerous things if you're not careful. They do say he'd been drinking heavily.'

'Yes, I suppose it must have been something like that.' Mott agreed readily, but he was quite certain that it hadn't been like that at all. This was the first of the chain of murders, and he thought he knew what must have happened. In his enforced retirement Blythe would have spent a lot of time poring over his books and photographs, and one day he might have spotted something which could lead to blackmail.

Yes, a man like Blythe would have enjoyed the thought of blackmail – of making somebody squirm. He would have written a letter, and waited for a reply with a good deal of pleasure and anticipation. But the reply never came. The victim called personally, and Blythe and his photographs went up in flames.

'And now, Mrs McDoggart, I think I'll get moving. You put the sandwiches I wanted into my pack? Good.' Mott crossed to the hatstand, and took down a haversack, a coil of rope, and a thick webbed belt from which hung a hammer and a collection of pitons – hardened steel spikes with eyeholes. With the belt round his waist and the pack on his back he looked like a particularly ferocious guerrilla leader. He nodded to his hostess and strode purposefully to the door.

The village of Glencarron stands at the top of a narrow valley, and all round it are the hills. To Mott's right lay the hump of the Bald Mountain, with the shoulder of Ben Nevis just visible behind it on the far horizon; to the left Sgurr Attow, topped by streaks of cloud; and straight ahead the black, scowling face of Ben Gael, the pine trees on its lower slopes giving way to heather, heather to scree, and finally the scree solidifying into rock. A great, towering wall of rock as smooth as a sheet of glass which seemed to cling to the mountain.

Then, as he drew nearer, the image changed, and he could make out the gullies and fissures which time had made in the rock. Towers and pinnacles clung to their sides, and half way to the summit lay the Flake itself, a hundred-foot ridge stretching across the cliff like the lip on a ravaged stone face.

Mott marched quickly up the valley, keeping to the side of a slate-coloured stream which roared like a distant train. The pitons in his belt jingled melodiously at each step, and he felt like a soldier marching to war; a great, happy soldier with victory assured – and those rock battlements above him were the towers of his enemy's castle. Only at the shell of the cottage where David Blythe had been burned to death did he pause, glancing briefly at the blackened walls and collapsed roof. There was nothing to be learned there, he decided. Fire and weather had done their work well, and Blythe and his photographs were dead and done with. He was almost on the point of marching on, when he felt he was being watched, and swung round on his heel.

The boy was sitting on a boulder to the left of the cottage, and he looked about fourteen. He wore tennis shoes, a faded khaki shirt, and torn flannels. There appeared to be something the matter with his face, for it was set in a mask of cold fury.

'Good morning, my lad.' By and large Mott liked boys. He usually found that they provided an excellent audience.

'You been doing a bit of scrambling, eh?' He waited for the set face to break into a smile of welcome, and some courteous Highland greeting to come from the pursed lips.

It didn't. If anything, the scowl became still deeper, and the boy's eyes remained fixed on Mott's belt. When he spoke his voice was like a verger's who has just discovered someone smoking in church.

'You'll no be using them, I trust?'

'Them?' Mott followed the direction of his gaze. 'Oh, you mean the pitons. Not unless I have to, my boy, but they're useful things when one's climbing alone. Just why do you hope I won't use them, though?'

'Because it's no sportin', that's why. The gentleman who was here last summer said it was no sportin'.'

'Not sporting!' Mott's face started to glow with anger. 'And just who was this – this gentleman?'

'Sir Roland Rawson, that's who it was. Taught me how to climb, he did. One of the best mountaineers in the world, Sir Roland is. Said that only vandals use pitons on British hills. All right on big mountains like the Alps, perhaps, but here it spoils the fun for other people; hammerin' the rock full of spikes.'

'Rawson, Roland Rawson!' Mott could hardly bring himself

to pronounce the name, for he and 'Rhino' Rawson had been enemies since boyhood: at school each struggling for the title of Victor Ludorum and cheating on the way; at university each striving to place chamber-pots on a higher steeple than the other, and both finally being sent down for it by a long-suffering but exasperated authority; in war vying for military glory with little concern for the safety of those under their command.

The final break had come three years back, when both claimed to have discovered the source of a certain African river. As it happened, both had been proved wrong by a young American equipped with a helicopter, but Rawson had been given the credit and a knighthood before the truth was revealed. Mott had never forgiven him that, and he wasn't allowed to forget it either. Each Christmas a vulgar card arrived at his door bearing greetings to *Mister* Moldon Mott from *Sir* Roland Rawson, C.B.E. For a moment he thought of telling this unpleasant youth a few home truths about his hero, and then better sense prevailed. Rawson and his creatures were beneath contempt. He turned away in disgust and pounded on towards the mountain.

But fury and injured dignity drove him forward like whips, and soon he was through the pines and the heather and clattering up across the screes. Plenty of recent scree-falls too, he noticed. The climbing guide was right. Most of the cliff was rotten, and would break away at a touch. All the same, that wouldn't hold him back. He wanted to trace the route of the Lents' last climb, and it would take more than a bit of loose rock to stop him. He'd damn well use pitons too, if he wanted. Who the hell was 'Rhino' Rawson to say what was unsporting or not? He pulled the guide-book from his pocket and checked the directions. 'The first pitch is fifty feet long, and begins at the top of the main scree slope. It is easily distinguished by a narrow ridge leading up to a broken tower.' Yes, that was right. He tightened his boot-laces, flexed his muscles, and began to climb.

Why does one climb a mountain? 'Because it's there,' said George Mallory. Because 'I have had a dream,' said Tenzing Norgay. 'For Germany,' said Toni and Adolf Schmidt, the Bavarian cyclists, and perhaps the greatest of them all. 'For the glory of J. Moldon Mott, and to run down a particularly unpleasant murderer,' thought Mott, and drove home his first piton. Unsportin' indeed! The cliff was loose and dangerous, and if he wanted to knock it full of spikes he'd do so.

All the same he made rapid progress, scrambling up over the ridges and towers and chimneys like an enormous ginger-coloured crab, and protecting himself with a loop of rope and a piton wherever necessary. It was still morning when at last he pulled himself up on to the Flake and lit a cigarette.

And from there the view was fantastic. Far away to the south, beyond the Ben Nevis massif, he could see a grey strip of water which was probably Loch Linnhe, and to the right, dwarfing Ben Gael, but dull and uninteresting by comparison, without the dignity of rock-falls or precipices, loomed the hump of the Bald Mountain. Straight in front of him stretched a long slope of heather and bracken from which David Blythe must have taken his photograph.

For quite a long time Mott lounged on the Flake, enjoying the view and his cigarette, and then he consulted the guide-book again. Apart from the dangers of loose rock, the route had been easy so far, but now came the crux – the problem which had sent Hal Lent spinning to his death more than fifty years ago. The Flake itself was a broken ledge stretching out over three hundred feet of air, and then tapering off into the cliff. Where it ended a deep chimney ran on to the summit, and was blocked by a chockstone – a boulder wedged between the walls of the chimney. And the chockstone was *swinging*, that was the point. It couldn't fall out, but a weight applied to it would make it tilt slightly till the walls of the chimney gripped it again. Quite easy if you were prepared and concentrating hard, but any lack of attention could lead to disaster.

'Well, here goes.' Mott prepared to move, but there was still an important piece of ritual to perform before he did so. Old climbers said it brought luck, and he was a firm believer in luck. He opened a zip fastener, and urinated noisily over the precipice. Then he started to creep forward across the Flake.

But it was easy – it was too damned easy. Even allowing for the fact that the rocks might have been icy, he couldn't see how that accident had occurred. All you had to do was to wedge yourself comfortably into the chimney, with your face looking out through its funnel towards the top of the Bald Mountain, and reach for the chockstone. As you put your weight on it, the stone tilted alarmingly but not dangerously, and came to rest. Then you pulled yourself over it, and the matter was finished. To an experienced climber the thing was far less dangerous than crossing a busy street. The idea of Hal Lent's being dragged off by a rope held by his brother was nonsense, too. The angles showed that he would merely have been pulled still deeper into the safety of the chimney. If Brother William had had murder in mind, he wouldn't have chosen that spot to try it.

No, there seemed no explanation for that accident, and for once Mott felt at a complete loss. Unless . . . !

Yes, unless, just as he grasped that swinging boulder, something had distracted him; a bird flying screaming out of its nest, for example. No, that was right out of the question. It was the wrong time of the year for nesting, and the rocks above were smooth and without fissure. No bird would have settled there.

He lowered himself back on to the Flake, and considered the problem. From just under the chockstone one was forced to look directly up through the chimney towards the summit of the Bald Mountain. Suppose – just suppose that, as Hal made his move, he had seen something on that summit; something that had made him start and slacken his grip as the stone began to move.

Mott drove home his last piton, and attached his rope to it in a running belay. Yes, that might be it. Just as the stone tilted Hal had seen something happen on the summit of the Bald Mountain, and for the fraction of a second he had stopped concentrating.

But what could he have seen? A puff of smoke as from a volcano, perhaps? That was ridiculous, of course, but would do as an example. He swung himself up, trying to imagine that he would see something, and concentrating, not on the chockstone, but on the bare hill above it. As before, his hands ran over the stone, but this time it was all quite different.

For, this time, he didn't feel it start to move. With his mind else-where he didn't notice that first, slow swing forward, and his hands missed their grip. For a second his fingers scrabbled against the rock, and his boots kicked at the walls of the chimney for a foot-hold, but it was too late. A sledge-hammer seemed to take him between the eyes and carry him down. The world exploded.

★   ★   ★

'The fellow must have a skull on him like a ruddy ape.' The words seemed to come from far away in the distance, and Mott forced his eyes open. Slowly the face of an old man with weather-beaten cheeks and a shock of white hair swam into focus.

'Aha, so you're coming round, me old son. And it's a lucky chap you are, it seems. Just a few bruises and a touch of concussion.' Dr Angus MacBain beamed at the figure on the couch. His son, the regular practitioner at Glencarron, had been out on a case when Mott was brought in, and he had taken charge.

'Now, let's see, shall we? Does this hurt you at all?' He gave his patient a sharp dig in the side, and was rewarded with a howl of pain and fury.

'It does, eh! Good, excellent, in fact. No damage to the nervous system then, and no bones broken either.

'It was your skull that saved you, of course. Why, in almost fifty years of medicine I don't think I've seen a thicker cranium. Really most interesting. A terrific knock you must have taken before the rope caught you up.' He pulled a chair and sat down beside the couch.

'Yes, we can thank your skull and young Billy Grant for saving your life, I think. Smart boy, Billy. It seems he was watching you on the climb, and ran for help when he saw you fall. The men got a party together and pulled you up like a trussed fowl. Aye, you should be grateful to young Billy. Without him you'd be as dead as a doornail.'

'I'm grateful.' Mott remembered the unpleasant youth who had accused him of being unsportin'. He also remembered just how he had come to fall from that chockstone, and he knew that his idea of murder was as dead as he might have been.

Yes, Hal Lent's death had been an accident all right. Something, probably something quite innocent, had distracted him as he reached for the stone, and that was all there was to it. All the same, he was quite certain there had been no accident about the way in which David Blythe had died. He would have to look for another motive that made *Grey Boulders* a reason for murder.

'I'm also most grateful to you,' he said. 'You're Dr MacBain, aren't you? And you gave up your fishing trip to attend to me.'

'Aye, that I did, Mr Mott, but don't let it bother you. My son was out on a case, so they sent over for me. One gets used to emergencies in a wild place like this, you know; climbing accidents and sick animals. Why, I've often regarded myself as much a vet as a doctor.'

'A vet!' Mott hadn't cared for the references to his skull, and his eyes gleamed at the thought of a possible insult. But there was nothing but good humour in MacBain's weather-beaten face.

'Can I get up now, doctor?'

'In a moment, in a moment, man, but don't let's hurry it. A rest won't do you any harm, and besides, I'm wanting to ask you a few questions. Just what is your interest in old Davie Blythe? Oh, aye, Mrs McDoggart at the inn told me you were interested all right.'

'Yes, I suppose she would have done.' Mott smiled slightly. 'A cousin of his, a Miss Bell, asked me to make some inquiries about him.' The lie came easily in spite of the pain in his head.

'I understand that you were about his only friend, doctor.'

'No, no, I wouldn't describe myself as a friend, Mr Mott.' MacBain's mop of white hair fluttered as he shook his head.

'Old Davie wasn't a man to have friends. No, he was far too bitter and sour for that. Felt that life had let him down and made him fail both as a priest and a photographer, which were the only two things he really wanted.

'He was quite an amusing old cuss though, when he wasn't feeling sorry for himself. Just what is this cousin's interest in him now, though? He's been dead quite a time.'

Mott told him the truth – or most of the truth. Not about

Roach, or the clerk at the publishers' office, but about the book and his suspicions that there was something hidden in it. There was something in MacBain's face that told him he might make a useful ally.

'Aye, so that's it, is it? And you've come to the right house, Mr Mott. You suspect there was something funny about Davie's death, do you? Well, so do I, and I've got my reasons for saying so, whatever my fool of a son may think.' The old eyes were very shrewd and thoughtful.

'No, we'll talk about my suspicions in a moment, but let's think about the book first – *The Grey Boulders*. It's a long time ago, of course, but I remember how pleased Davie was when the publishers took three of his pictures for it. There was one of the Tower Ridge on Ben Nevis, one of the Coolin Hills, and this one of Ben Gael, with the Lent brothers on the Flake just before the accident.

'A bit of luck his getting that. He told me how excited he was when he developed the print and saw the figures on the mountain.'

'What's that you say?' Mott jerked himself up into a sitting position. 'You mean he didn't know he had taken them at the time?'

'No, of course he didn't. The camera had been left out on the hills for over a week with a trip wire attached to the trigger. Davie was after getting a photograph of a mountain hare. He did, too. One of them crossed the wire and set it off. You could see the beast's backside in the very corner of the picture. It was cut out of the published version, of course.'

'I see. And you're sure about this, doctor? You're quite certain that's how the photograph was taken?' This might have no bearing at all on the story, but Mott was suddenly very interested.

'Of course I'm sure.' MacBain flushed with annoyance. 'I may be old, but my memory's as good as ever, whatever my son says.

'Besides, I remember the year he took that picture well. It was the last time we were allowed to burn the Butcher.'

'To burn the Butcher!' Mott's eyebrows came up in a bar across his forehead.

'Aye, the Butcher – Butcher Cumberland – William, Duke of Cumberland, who put down the last Scottish rising at Culloden in

1746. It was the old laird, Sir Archibald's grandfather, who started it. A queer, mad family, the Bethunes, but an amusing bunch for all that. The old man was a Scottish nationalist and thought that the House of Hanover was responsible for most of our troubles. On each anniversary of his death we used to carry the Butcher up to the top of the Bald Mountain and sit him on a bonfire.'

'Oh, I see. You mean burn him in effigy?'

'Of course in effigy! The damned fellow died in 1765.' MacBain frowned. He'd heard that this Mott was something of a personage, but his head really did seem thick in both senses of the term.

'Aye, grand times we used to have at the Butcher's burnings; dancing round the fire on the top of the mountain, and singing, and letting off rockets. Then we'd all come down to the village, and drink toasts to Scotland, and Edward Stuart, the King across the water.'

'And 1909 was the last time this happened?'

'That it was, I'm sorry to say. Some busybody got up in Parliament, and said it was an insult to the present Royal Family and should be stopped. They stationed police round the mountain the next year.' There was a sudden sadness in the doctor's eyes, as he remembered the joys of his youth.

'Oh, we had some fine times at the Butcher's burnings.'

'I bet you did. But to get back to Blythe, Doctor. Just what makes you think there was something odd about his death?'

'I've two reasons, Mr Mott, and the first is purely circumstantial, and may mean nothing at all.' MacBain tilted back his chair and crossed his legs.

'All the same, I was with old Davie a few hours before the fire started, and I can tell you he was cold sober, and there was no drink in the house. He brought out his only bottle when I called, and there was barely enough whisky in it to give us each a dram. He was a careful man, too; not the sort of man to go knocking over a lamp.

'Aye, I remember that evening like it was yesterday. We discussed wills.'

'Wills!' Mott craned forward, and he remembered how Roach

and Marsden had died. 'You mean he might have been considering suicide?'

'Indeed I do not. What man would be fool enough to kill himself by fire? No, not his own will at all. Just wills in general, and crazy ones in particular. He had been reading a book on the subject, he said; *Tied-Up Riches*, I think it was called; about wills with silly conditions in 'em. You know the kind of thing well enough. "I leave everything to my dear wife, providing she wears mourning for the rest of her life." "A thousand quid to Cousin George if he undertakes to push a wheelbarrow from London to Glasgow in three days." David was pretty amusing about it. I don't think I'd ever seen him in a better mood.'

'No, I can imagine that.' As he listened a picture had begun to grow in Mott's head. An unpleasant, spiteful old man reading a book on eccentric wills, and suddenly remembering something he had noticed in a photograph taken by a trip wire a long time ago. As far as Hal Lent was concerned, there had been no hint of murder, but there might be the start of a new theory.

'And your second reason, doctor?'

'My second reason is not circumstantial, Mr Mott, but based on knowledge and observation.' MacBain got up and crossed to a bench by the surgery door. He pulled over a Bunsen burner, and lit it.

'My son said I was just an old fool, of course, and the police doctor from Inverness backed him up. Told me I should never have even been allowed to look at the corpse.' He picked up a sheet of paper and held it just out of reach of the flame. It curled and started to darken before he pulled it aside.

'Well, I'm no fool, Mr Mott. They were the fools, and they didn't even use their eyes.

'Oh, yes, David Blythe was burned to death all right, and an oil lamp may well have been turned over. All the same, any doctor worth his salt should be able to distinguish between burns, you know. A naked flame chars, and withers the flesh evenly, like this piece of paper I'm holding. But a pressure burn – from a length of hot iron, for instance – leaves a scar, a ridge in the tissue. And

I found such scars, Mr Mott. On the soles of both his feet I found them.' He twisted the paper into a ball and threw it aside.

'No, I couldn't prove anything, and both my fool of a son and the police surgeon told me to mind my own business. All the same, to the best of my knowledge old Davie had been tortured before he died.'

Twelve

'No, Mrs Brassey, I'm very sorry, but I just can't use these.' John shook his head and started to push the books back into the worn suitcase.

'It isn't that they're bad books, but I've far too much ordinary stock on my shelves at the moment. If I bought these they'd be taking shelf-room from books I know I can sell.'

'But, Mr Cain, these are good books. I know that, because my husband bought them, and he was a great collector; he knew what he was doing all right.' The woman was old and tired, and looked ill. Everything about her, from the worn shoes to the pinched face, spoke of better days that had ended a long time ago.

'And some of them came from your shop, Mr Cain. That's your price mark, isn't it?'

'Yes, that's my mark.' John glanced at the pencilled scribble on the fly-leaf of *Sixty Years a Queen*. For a moment he thought of sending her to Newby's bookshop round the corner, and then thought better of it.

In the first place he knew that ten minutes later he would have to listen to George Newby's rasping voice on the telephone saying, 'Thanks, Johnnie. Thanks very much indeed for sending me that old bag, with her load of rubbish. Just you wait and see what I'm going to send you next week, chum.'

In the second place, he remembered Brassey well; a little, nervous man – a retired schoolmaster probably – who came into the shop at least once a week and went out proudly clutching a book one was delighted to see the back of.

Well, Brassey was dead now, and had left his widow nothing but memories, and debts, and a bookcase of worthless volumes which he had imagined were bargains. Now the gas, or the light, or the coal bill was long overdue, and she had pulled out a little pile of them, thinking she had at least some capital.

'But you see, it's like this, Mrs Brassey – ' He started to explain the working of the business – that one only bought the run-of-the-mill books because one had to, because among a pile of rubbish there might be a few saleable items and one had to take the lot to get them; that the rest, the lumber, would sit on the shelves for a time in the hope of finding a mug, and then be tied up in sacks and sent away for pulp.

'And I've got a lot more at home, Mr Cain,' she broke in. 'If you would only buy these, you can come up and look at the rest any time you want. My husband knew what he was doing, and I'm sure you'd find some *first editions.*' Like most of the uninformed public, she used the term 'first edition' as though it were some kind of lucky charm or talisman.

'I'm sure I might, Mrs Brassey, but – ' He pulled out the books and studied the titles again. *Lloyd George's War Memoirs, With the Flag to Pretoria, The Works of Sir Walter Scott, Bart*, contained in two heavy, unmanageable volumes of tiny print; *Rogers' Poetry* – that was quite a pretty binding, but who read Rogers these days? Junk, just junk to clutter his shelves.

'No, I'm very sorry – ' he began to say; then he saw the despair in her face, and knew that he had been her last hope – that if he didn't buy, she would realize that her husband was just a fool who had bought books merely because they looked important and pretentious.

'All right, then, three pounds,' he said, and he knew that he was a failure as he said it. There was no room for sentiment in trade, and if he carried on like this he wouldn't be long in business. He pulled the notes from his till, and watched her pick up the suitcase and walk away with an odd hint of pride in her step. She obviously thought he was a crook who had first decried the books to get them cheap, and her late husband's knowledge was justified.

'Damn her!' he thought. 'Damn everybody!' He stacked his worthless purchases on the side of the desk, and then went through into the back room. If he was lucky he would make a profit of ten shillings in about three months' time, not counting overheads.

'Ah, back again, old boy. Any luck?' Mott sat beside the table, and though it was a warm day he was dressed in tweeds. There was a shepherd's crook propped up beside him, and a long strip of sticking plaster ran across his forehead. A good deal of the usual bounce seemed to have left him.

'No, no luck at all. Now, just what was the title you wanted me to check?' John took a strip of paper from him and frowned.

'No, he's got that wrong, I'm afraid. All the same, I think I know the book. Hang on a second.' He went back into the shop and a moment later returned bearing a slim, modern volume. 'Could this be it?'

'Yes, I think that's the joker all right.' Mott eased himself cautiously forward and looked at the book. It had a very gay dust-wrapper showing a hand holding a quill pen above a sheet of parchment, and the title read, *Riches with strings attached, An account of various eccentric wills and legacies*, by Vernon H. Johnston.

'Now, let's see what Mr Johnston can tell us. That fellow Blythe was very interested by his book, and I wonder if it will be of any interest to us.' Mott turned over the endpapers and frowned.

'No, no damned index of course. I'll just have to work through it. Yes, "Enforced Widows", "The Tankerton Estate", "Follies and Memorials – " Blah, blah! Nothing for us so far.' With his fist propped under his big chin he looked like an unpleasant caricature of Rodin's 'Thinker'.

Then all at once his expression altered. It creased into a deep frown of concentration, and his eyebrows came up in a bar across his forehead, while a low whistle broke from his lips.

'Yes, got you!' he said, and his face was a beaming mask of triumph.

'Oh, my giddy aunt, Cain! I really think we're home at last – home and dry! Thank you, Mr Vernon Johnston! You're a lousy writer, but I'm very, very grateful.' He closed the book with a snap as John leaned over his shoulder.

'Oh no, old boy, not just for a minute. I think I know the truth now, but I want to prove it first. Have you got a *Dictionary of Dates* about the place?

'Good. Then this is what I'd like you to do.' He scribbled a question on a sheet of paper. 'Get on to the Record Office and ask them this. They hate answering questions on the phone, so you'll have to be firm. Tell them it's a matter of life and death; three deaths at the very minimum. First get me that dictionary and a magnifying glass, though.

'Thanks.' He watched John lift the phone, and then pulled the copy of *Grey Boulders* from his pocket, not opening it at once, but smiling down at the tooled binding.

'Well, my dear,' he said, 'you're just about the last member of your family left, so are you going to talk now? Are you going to tell me what really happened? Yes, Chapter Eight I think it was – page ninety-five.' He opened the book, and started to read, muttering the words aloud.

'"My brother and I had been camping out on the hills for a week before the accident happened",' he read. '"It was our intention to stay in the district for about a fortnight, and attempt to climb every important precipice between Ben Nevis and Sla n'Avail."'

Yes, that fitted all right. That was the first piece of the jigsaw he needed, and there were just two more to go. Two little scraps of information which would tell him the name of a killer.

Very slowly he turned to the photograph of that last climb of the Lent Brothers. There was the cliff, looking as smooth and unbroken as he had seen it in the distance. There were the figures of the climbers like tiny dots against the rock; Hal below the chockstone which had killed him, and William staring out over the valley. And in the distance lay the hump of the Bald Mountain topped by a cairn, and a little drifting cloud. It was at that hump that Hal had been looking just before he fell.

And there was something very wrong about the photograph. It had been taken by a camera left out on the hills for days, and set off when a mountain hare had touched a trip wire. By pure chance it showed two climbers just before a fatal accident, but that wasn't the important thing about it. The important thing was that it showed something which had no right to be there, but which a vicious old man had noticed after reading a book on peculiar wills and legacies.

Very slowly Mott picked up the magnifying glass and held it over the photograph, and as he did so, he knew that he was right at last – completely right. For there was no cairn on the top of the Bald Mountain, and there never had been. What looked like a cairn was a blazing bonfire with figures dancing round it, and the cloud above was smoke from the fire. 'The last time we burned the Butcher.' He pushed the book away from him and opened Haydn's *Dictionary of Dates*.

'Well, that's that, Cain. That clinches it, I think.' He took the paper John handed him, and looked at the answer to his question. It was just as he had expected, and there was no more doubt in his mind.

'Yes, your first theory was correct, it seems. There is a mad collector at work, but he doesn't only collect books. He collects money; such a lot of money.' For the last time Mott pulled over the little blue volume and stared at the figures of the climbers. This time it was not Hal, but William on the Flake below who interested him.

'You old devil,' he said very quietly, and there was nothing but admiration in his eyes.

'Yes, you clever, brave, old devil. You did what you thought was right, and you almost succeeded. Yes, if the Duke of Cumberland hadn't died on a thirteenth of October, you'd have got away with it.'

* * *

'I think he's better, Miss Julia; a little better. In his body, that is.' Peter Trew greeted her at the top of the long, curved staircase, and he looked terrible. There were dark lines under his eyes, and his thin, nondescript features were pinched and drawn. His suit was crumpled, as though he had been trying to sleep in it.

'But his mind, Miss! I'm worried about his mind. When the doctors told him he must never go to the office again, never even open a business letter, I think he felt he was as good as dead.'

'I know that, Peter. I think I felt the same.' Julia bowed her head slightly.

'And, in a way, I suppose he is. Apart from the firm he's never had any interests or hobbies, has he? Not even any close friends, except you. I suppose it's natural enough, too. When you're holding down an empire, you don't have time for friends or hobbies. But now the empire has been taken out of his hands and there's nothing left.'

'No, nothing but memories, Miss Julia. Memories, and yourself, of course.'

'Me? Oh, I see what you mean. He'll want me to try and take an active part in the business now. Well, I'm very sorry, but that's out of the question, and it's better to tell him so right away.' She started to walk towards the bedroom door, and then turned and looked back at Trew.

'Peter,' she said, 'I want to ask you something. You remember how the attack took him at the beginning. Do you think it could have been anything to do with that book he wanted that brought it on?'

'The book?' Trew frowned slightly, as though considering. 'Yes, he was upset, wasn't he, but I don't think that what he said meant anything. It seemed to me he was delirious before he fainted. I asked the doctor about it afterwards. He told me that in the Chief's state of health almost anything could have brought on the attack. Even a trivial disappointment like not getting a book he wanted.'

'I see. Thanks, Peter. And don't worry, I'll be very gentle with him.' She pulled open the door and walked into the bedroom.

Sir Stephen Lent lay on a big, canopied bed, and his thin body hardly raised a bulge under the blankets. His face was almost the colour of the pillow, and whatever Peter Trew might say, he didn't look even physically better.

'Ah, there you are, Julia. Sit down and talk to me, will you? The doctors have said that I may have one or two social visitors at last.'

'Yes, they told me you seemed better.' She bent down and kissed his cheek that felt as cold and lifeless as paper, and then pulled a chair up beside the bed. Like all the furniture in the room it was heavy and ornate, and had been in the family for years.

'Oh, they said I seemed better, did they? Well, perhaps they are right. Perhaps with care and strict attention to nothing I may lie here for years.' The tired eyes flickered round the room over the dark, Victorian furniture; mahogany tables, and oak chests of drawers, and polished tallboys which stood like symbols of the philosophy of possession.

' "Yes, if you only take things easy, Sir Stephen, there's no reason why you shouldn't reach ninety – a few months in Switzerland, or a long sea voyage perhaps – " Rubbish! Fruit left lying rots quickly, and whatever my medical advisers tell you, I won't see another Christmas.' There was no bitterness in his voice, only blank acceptance, as though noting some unpleasant but quite trivial fact.

'No, death has given me too much rope already, and I should have gone out in the office the other day. You'll be the last of the family soon, Julie. A rather doomed family, it seems to be. I'll be one of the few of us to die in bed like a gentleman. Your father killed in that motoring accident. My two sons blown to pieces at Arnhem and Cassino. Old Hal Lent, your grandfather, falling off that Scottish mountain, and William following him twenty years later when a boiler exploded at the Coventry plant.'

'Uncle, need we talk quite so much about death? You're beginning to depress me.'

'Oh, I'm sorry, my dear. I don't want to do that.' As though with a tremendous effort the old face twisted itself into a smile.

'You've been depressed and bored a lot, I think, Julie, but that's all finished now. Tomorrow morning the lawyers are coming here, and I'm making over control of the firm to you. It's been yours on paper for a long time, of course, though you didn't know it.

'Yes, six years ago I registered ninety per cent of my shares in your name, and that's enough to pay off my death duties, and leave you in control. No, you didn't know it, my dear. You just thought you were signing a dividend warrant at the time. All the same, you know now, and you've got to learn all about the business, because you're a Lent, and it belongs to you. Use your power well, Julie.'

'I'll try to, Uncle.' She turned away from his cold face, and she couldn't tell him what she intended to do: that as soon as he died, her shares would be put up on the stock market; that she had no interest in the business. She knew quite well that the knowledge would kill him as easily as a knife through the heart.

'Yes, you're going to be a very powerful woman, my dear. Thirteen factories now, mineral concessions in four continents, forty ships in the fleet, nineteen thousand employees on the pay-roll last year – ' Like a gramophone record the voice ran on, reciting the list of their possessions, and as she listened a wilderness seemed to stretch away before Julia's eyes – a nightmare world of boardroom doors being opened for her, and balance sheets being read to her, and an army of feet marching across the earth to provide her with yachts, and jewels, and Riviera villas, but never bringing the security she craved. She was a passionate woman, but still a virgin, for she knew that just at the moment of pleasure she would hear a cold, familiar voice saying, 'No, it's not you, my sweet. It isn't you he wants, but just your cheque book.'

'Please, Uncle,' she said. 'Please don't talk about it. You're going to live a long time, and in any case I know nothing about the business.'

'But you're going to learn, my dear. Peter Trew will teach you. You can rely on Peter, for he and his family have been with us for a long time. Yes, since our first plant was opened at Gravesend, the Lents and the Trews have stood together. You can always trust Peter, Julie.'

'I know that, but shouldn't you rest now, Uncle?' Julia frowned as she looked at the face on the pillow. He really was terribly ill.

'Rest! No, I don't want to rest. I'll have plenty of time for that soon, my girl, and don't you forget it.' A little of the old fire which could crush a boardroom revolt in seconds, or browbeat a strike delegation, had crept back into his voice.

'Whatever those fools of doctors may tell you, I know I'm dying, and I want to get everything in order first. Those shares were made over early enough to stop the tax people ruining us, and tomorrow morning you'll be in control. You've got to promise me something first, though, Julie. Yes, you've got to give me a promise.' As though the last spark of authority had tired him, his voice was very weak now, and the lips were barely moving.

'Promise you what, Uncle?' Julia craned forward to make out the words. They seemed to come from far away in the distance, as though she were alone with a dead man, and somebody else was speaking to her through the wall.

'That you'll never sell stock – our stock. We never have done in the past, you know, and not one penny piece of the business belongs to anyone outside the family. And you're the family now, my dear, so promise me you won't sell. Yes, since Fords put their shares on the market, we're one of the few really big private concerns left now. In that way we control not just money and stock, but the company, Julie – our company. We took the name "Allied" when we bought up other firms, but it's still "Lent Engineering" when you get to rock bottom – still our own business. Yes, for a hundred years it's been our business. Not a bad record.'

'All right. I promise not to sell, Uncle.' She looked away from the bed for a moment. There was something both pathetic and horrible in the sight of that dying man striving to keep control of the company in the hands of a family whose last surviving member didn't want it.

'Good, good.' Lent nodded his head on the pillow, and then his eyes started to close, as though he felt he had earned the right to rest at last.

'Yes, yes, you're a good, sensible girl, Julie, and you mustn't worry any more. Yes, by tomorrow we'll have got the last one, and that wretched book won't be able to hurt us.' The lips stopped moving, and something he had been holding against the sheet slipped from his fingers and fell to the floor.

'The book! But, Uncle, what about the book? Just how can it hurt us, and why should I be worried about it?' Memories of all John and Mott had told her raced through Julia's mind, and she was suddenly frightened. Was she herself somehow involved in Roach's death?

'Please, Uncle, you've got to let me know.'

But it was no use. Lent was fast asleep now, lying as peacefully as a child, and it would be murder to wake him. She leaned forward and picked up the thing he had dropped. It was a tastefully got-up catalogue from the Compton Gallery, with the final item, a copy of *Grey Boulders*, underlined in red ink.

Thirteen

'FIFTY-FIVE – sixty – Thank you, sir, eighty then. Eighty I am bid for a signed first edition of Herman Melville's *The Whale*. Any advance on eighty for this extremely rare book with the author's inscription on the title-page? Going – going – sold then.' Mr Gordon Angel's ivory hammer tapped sharply on the desk, and the clerk beside him made an entry in his ledger.

'Sold to Mr Nigel Camp of New York City, for five hundred and eighty pounds. That is seventeen hundred and twenty-four dollars, sir.' He mopped his brow with a tasteful silk handkerchief as a porter held up a volume of the next lot.

Yes, not a bad price for the Melville, he thought. Not bad at all, and the sale was going well as a whole. The room was nicely filled, and not just with London dealers, but the foreign trade too, and quite a sprinkling of private collectors. He could see Lord Cranton leaning against a wall by the doorway, for instance. The old boy looked as though he hadn't got a penny to bless himself with, but he owned one of the few important private libraries left in the country.

Then there was this fellow Camp who'd bought the last lot; been spending a lot of money on this trip. Probably most of it would be from customers who'd commissioned him to buy for them, but he must have a very nice stock of his own. He'd heard that the title 'Golden Volumes' over his Manhattan store wasn't just an idle boast.

Yes, the sale was going very well, and the presence of foreigners and private buyers prevented any interference from the Ring. The 'boys' couldn't operate against that kind of competition. He glanced at the silent little group, consisting of Goldsmith, Burton, and Callaghan, standing to the right of his desk. Bless their stony little hearts, he thought. There wouldn't be any dividend today.

Yes, the sale was going nicely, and only one thing worried Angel:

that last lot he'd put in to help that wretched fellow Cain. Still, who the hell was Cain, anyway? If the man had any sense at all he'd be delighted with the new arrangement. All the same, he supposed he should have asked him first. No, of course it would be all right. He pushed aside all unpleasant thoughts, and beamed at his audience.

'And now, ladies and gentlemen, we come to what is without any doubt the most important item of the day. A set of Gould's *Humming Birds* in fine condition, apart from a little foxing on the end-papers.

'Yes, it's a long time since I had the pleasure of selling a Gould, so what may I start at? A thousand pounds? Eight hundred then? Thank you, my lord.' He nodded, as Cranton raised a gnarled finger.

'Eight hundred pounds I am bid for –'

'Only two more lots to go.' From their group at the side of the room, Mott, John and Julia were thinking the same thing. As soon as Angel had disposed of two more lots, *Grey Boulders* would be put up, and the murderer might reveal himself. They looked forward to that with mixed feelings. John's were a mixture of excitement and dread. He still didn't completely believe Mott's theory, but there was a good deal of evidence to support it. If it was true, then he realized that somebody he had become fond of was going to be badly hurt, and he didn't want that – no, he didn't want it at all.

Julia's feelings, on the other hand, were made up of dumb misery and acceptance. She had not the slightest idea what secret the book might contain, but she was quite certain that her family were somehow caught up in it. She wanted to know the truth, but she also feared it. Although the room was warm and she wore furs, she felt terribly cold.

Only Mott appeared unconcerned. Like an impatient Roman emperor waiting for the Christians to enter the arena and the real fun to begin, he leaned on his crook and stared scornfully across the room. In a few minutes he was certain that the person who had killed Roach, and Blythe, and Marsden would show his hand, and the matter would be finished. He had not the slightest doubt that his theory was correct in every detail, and what remained was merely a mopping-up operation.

'Sold then – sold to Mrs Laura K. Richardson of – ? Thank you, madam – of Weston, Massachusetts – for one thousand, four hundred pounds – ' The urbane, syrupy voice of Gordon Angel broke into his thoughts, and Mott scowled at him. The fellow really was a slow-moving pomposity. A great, foolish ox of a man, with an ox's dewlaps hanging down over his wing collar, and a great, draped belly bulging across the desk. Why couldn't the fellow hurry up? Mott would have loved to plant a fist in the very centre of that belly.

'And now, ladies and gentlemen, we come to a set of Hakluyt's *Voyages*, very nicely bound in full red morocco.' Angel paused and blew his nose with unnecessary violence, as though deliberately wasting time, before starting the bidding.

But the sale of the Hakluyt didn't take long. In comparison with the other lots it was unimportant, and only three bids were needed to knock it down to a London bookseller. Mott craned forward eagerly as Angel consulted his catalogue; staring across the room as though hoping to recognize the face of his suspect before the bidding started.

And there was something wrong, it seemed – yes, something was very wrong. No porter appeared, holding up the copy of *Grey Boulders* for inspection, and Angel didn't call out the lot number. Instead, he took a sip of water, and stood up.

'Well, my friends, I think that concludes our business,' he said. 'All that there remains for me to do is to thank you one and all for your support. Our practice of holding sales on a Saturday afternoon has become quite a feature of the Compton Gallery of late, and I'm sure you will agree that –

'What's that, Fred?' He frowned, and leaned across to his clerk.

'Oh, yes, of course.' For a moment they whispered together, and then Angel cleared his throat and addressed the room. 'Ladies and gentlemen,' he said blandly, 'with regard to the final lot advertised in our catalogue, the Trefoil Press edition of a book entitled *The Grey Boulders*: at the last moment it was withdrawn on the instructions of the owner. I really must apologize about – '

'What the devil!' Mott's bellow of rage and astonishment rang across the room, and his hand gripped John's arm like a vice.

'Just what's happened, Cain? What went wrong? You didn't tell him to withdraw it, did you?'

'No, of course I didn't. I gave him our instructions, and he promised to carry them out to the letter.' John shook his arm free, and there was nothing but bewilderment in his face.

'Somebody must have got to him before the sale started.'

'Yes, I suppose they must. Well, we're going to see about that, and Mr Gordon Angel is going to get a lesson he won't forget in a hurry. Excuse me, madam – out of my way, sir.' With John at his heels, and pushing aside all who blocked their way, Mott strode forward to the desk. His face was a great red ball of indignation, and he brandished his shepherd's crook like a weapon.

'Now, Mr Gordon Angel, just what explanation have you to offer? I happen to be the owner of that book, and I gave no instructions for its withdrawal. Come on, man, answer me.'

From her place by the wall Julia watched them. It might have been a scene from an early slap-stick movie. For a moment Angel faced Mott bravely enough, a bishop defying the pagan hordes from his altar steps, and then he turned with a squeak of terror and bolted for a door like an enormous black rabbit. Mott started after him, and almost involuntarily the crook seemed to leap forward, catch him round the ankle, and drag him to earth with a crash that shook the room. From every side came screams and shouts, and three porters hurled themselves on top of Mott. Julia stared fascinated, and then turned with a start as a hand gripped her arm.

'Will you come with me, please, Miss Julia.' The voice at her side was very urgent.

'Yes, it's bad news, I'm afraid – the very worst. Your uncle is dead, and it's time you learned the truth at last,' said Peter Trew.

* * *

'Yes, sergeant, most certainly I intend to prefer charges. What-ever mistake I made, it's an outrage.' Angel lay back on a sofa in his office, and he didn't look urbane or pompous any more. His coat was torn, and already his right eye, which had collided with the door-knob, was starting to blacken. He looked like a great grey fish that has been left too long on the slab.

'Oh, I may have exceeded your instructions by selling the book privately, Cain, but I did it in your best interests. Two hundred pounds in cash I got for a book which isn't worth twelve. And then you come here, and I am attacked by this – this.' He stared at Mott with a mixture of terror and indignation.

'And in public too – in the gallery itself – in front of everyone.' He raised his hand as though to wipe away a tear. 'I'll never be able to hold my head up again.'

'Why, you puffed-up nobody!' Mott appeared to be on the point of attacking him again, but was restrained by the policemen who stood at his side.

'Your reputation has nothing to do with it. All that concerns us is what happened to the book – my book, Mr Angel, which was entrusted to you to be put up for public auction.' His hand crashed against a table to drive home the point.

'Just what happened to that book?'

'But I was going to tell you, if you'd only give me the chance. I sold it. About an hour before the sale started, a man came up to me and asked if he could buy it privately. We'd never normally do business that way, of course, but the price he offered, Cain! Two hundred pounds in cash! I had to accept that kind of offer. I thought you'd be pleased.'

'Yes, normally I suppose I would have been pleased, Mr Angel – very pleased.' John leaned back against the wall, feeling utter weariness, and he knew that they had lost. That must have been the last copy of *Grey Boulders*, and the killer had got away with it, just as he always got away with it.

'But did you know the man? Did he tell you his name?' Even as he asked the question he knew that it was useless.

'No, I've never seen him before. Told me his name was Smith, but I didn't believe him. Said he was the agent of a rich collector who didn't mind what he paid but hated the publicity of an auction.

'But surely you know him, Cain? Yes, he was in the sale room today. That young lady you were with. I saw him go over and speak to her just as – as – ' Once again fear and indignation mingled in Angel's face, and he stared at Mott.

'The young lady!' Click – click – click! Like a metal puzzle the pieces started to snap together in John's head, and he knew that the theory he dreaded was coming true.

Yes, Julia, she was the key. She was the one that everything hinged on. But where was Julia? They'd left her in the sale room, but that was a quarter of an hour ago. Surely she should have followed them by now. Disregarding Mott's bellow of protest, he started to hurry out of the room, and then stopped dead in his tracks, as a tall, gaunt figure barred his way. It appeared to be dressed entirely in sackcloth, and held a pair of women's gloves in a claw-like hand.

'Good day to you, Mr Cain.' Lord Cranton beamed on him like an Israelite viewing the Promised Land for the first time.

'Sorry to butt in, but I just wanted to pop round and thank your friend for his performance. Haven't enjoyed myself so much for years. Did he manage to damage the fellow at all?' He bowed to Mott over John's shoulder, stared at Angel's recumbent figure on the couch, and burst into a cackle of senile glee.

'Yes, I see he did. Good for you, sir – excellent, in fact! Nasty, pompous chap, Angel! Always hated him since he made me lose a first of Willie Maugham's *Painted Veil*. The genuine first it was, too, with the Hong Kong libel passages left intact; very scarce book, as you well know, I dare say. He didn't even bother to send me the catalogue, though he knew I've been after a copy for years.

'By the way, you do remember me, Mr Cain? Been in your shop many times, but never managed to find anything I wanted so far. The name's Cranton.' He lifted his hand to shake John's and then stared in bewilderment at the gloves as though they were some sinister fungoid growth which had suddenly attached itself to him. Then his face cleared, and another childish cackle came from his lips.

'Yes, of course, how stoopid of me. Knew there was something else. Your friend, the young woman, dropped these as she went out. Silly of her, rushin' out like that and missin' all the fun. Never had much use for women meself. Anyway, here they are. Now, I'd like to make the acquaintance of the gentleman who gave friend Angel his deserts.' He started to shoulder his way towards Mott, but John put out his arm.

'Just a minute, please, Lord Cranton. You say she went out. Was she alone?'

'Alone?' The aged face almost cracked in its struggle to concentrate.

'No, not alone. There was a man with her. Common-looking little fellow, but I've seen him somewhere. Yes, that's right, in one of the financial papers it must have been. He's some kind of industrialist, I think. Name of Pew, or Trew, I seem to remember. Anyway, I thought it was odd at the time. The gel was cryin', and he was telling her that some relative or other had died, and they had to go to Gravesend.'

'To Gravesend! You're sure about that, Lord Cranton?'

'Sure? No, of course I'm not sure, young man. Not sure about anything these days.' He frowned impatiently.

'Think he said Gravesend, though. Place down the Thames, ain't it? Kent, I think it is. And now I want to shake hands with your friend and thank him for the way he served Angel.' Once again Cranton shook with mirth, but there was nobody to listen to him. John gave one final glance at Mott, who was struggling between the two policemen, and then ran through the sale room to his car.

Fourteen

FROM where they stood the Thames was a grey trickle, and London a toy town spread out on the horizon. Through the smoke haze that covered it, Julia could just make out the tiny dome of Saint Paul's cathedral, the Tower Bridge looking like matchsticks, and far away in the distance the television masts on the Surrey hills.

'Well, Peter,' she said, 'Why? Just why have you brought me here? You told me that Uncle was dead – that he had another stroke soon after I left for the sale – but why are we here? Why didn't you take me home?' She stood with Trew on the top of the new administration block at the Gravesend factory which Stephen Lent had resisted building for years, and her mind was reeling. Nothing fitted together any more, nothing made sense any more. Only Peter Trew seemed to exist, with his white face staring at her, and a thin strand of dark hair moving across his forehead in the wind.

'Well, why, Peter? Why are we here?' He had almost dragged her out of the sale room to the car, and driven down to Gravesend hardly speaking a word on the way. Now they stood at the top of the unfinished building which towered forty storeys above the flat landscape.

'You said something about telling me the truth at last – that there was something I had to know. But why here? Why bring me here?'

'Because this is the best place to show you, Julia. To make you understand what we had to do.' Trew's voice was just the same as ever, but his words lacked something. He no longer used the formal 'Miss'.

'Yes, look down, Julia – look all around you, and you'll understand. Old Martin Lent's first factory, and what we made of it. What a hundred years of sweat, and devotion, and genius have made of it.' His hand circled over the factory below them. White cooling-towers glinting in the sun, quays jutting out into the estu-

ary, and everywhere the dark roofs of warehouses and workshops.
It was deserted on the Saturday afternoon, and might have been
some dead, abandoned city on a forgotten planet. As she looked at
it, Julia was suddenly reminded of a Gospel quotation: 'The devil
taketh him unto an exceeding high mountain, and showeth him all
the kingdoms of the world, and the glory of them.'

'Yes, that's power, isn't it, Julia?' Trew's voice seemed to blend
with the wind, and sounded quite inhuman; reeds rustling beside
a lake.

'Real power, my dear. Not just stocks or shares, or money in the
bank, but something to control and use. Something worth fighting
for, I think – even worth killing for. And I saved it all for you, Julia
Lent.'

'Killing for!' Julia moved back a little from the parapet, and fear
was around her like a physical gas. Deep down in her mind she
seemed to remember that there was supposed to be some secret
in the family; something which was revealed to each member who
was ready to take an active part in the business. It seemed that she
was in that position now.

'Peter,' she said, 'I want you to tell me the whole story, and tell
it quickly.'

'I'll tell you, Julia. Didn't I bring you here to tell you? To the
one place where I'd be sure you'd understand.' Apart from the
lack of 'Miss', there was still subservience in Trew's voice; still the
servant-mistress relationship she had always known.

'I can't tell you quickly though, I'm afraid. It's a long story, you
know, and we have to go right back to the beginning – right back
to old Martin Lent who built this factory in the eighteen seventies.
But let's get out of the wind for a moment.' Trew drew her into
the shelter of a little open hut that stood behind them, and pulled
a single sheet of paper from his brief-case.

'You see, my dear, since 1909 your family have never owned one
brick or stone of all this business.' He smiled slightly at the doubt
in her face.

'Oh, yes, it's true all right, and I can prove it.' He handed her
the paper as though it were a routine business document. This is

a copy of old Martin's will, and if you read it carefully, you should begin to understand.'

'Thank you.' Julia frowned at the paper. Even in the shelter of the hut it fluttered slightly, and the archaic wording troubled her from time to time.

'I, Martin Lent, of the County of Sussex, being of sound mind do will and bequeath – ' Instructions for his funeral, gifts to servants, friends and charities. And at the end the things that mattered.

'To my sons, Hal and William, I leave my lands at Silver Beach, Gravesend, together with the factory situate thereon, provided always that the following conditions are observed and carried out – '

'But I know all this, Peter,' she said, and handed it back to him. 'I've seen a copy of the will before. He left the firm equally to Hal and William when they reached the age of thirty. If either of them died before that, it went out of the survivor's control. The old man had some mad idea that identical twins were too interdependent on each other, and if one died young, the other would crack up and ruin the business. There was also some clause about bankruptcy.'

'There was, Julia, but that need not concern us at all. Four years after old Martin died, coal deposits were discovered in the district, and the value of the factory went up by over three hundred per cent. No, there was no question of bankruptcy after that, and Hal and William were rich men.' Trew might have been a company secretary reading the balance sheet in his chairman's absence.

'No, it's the first clause that matters: that, if either son failed to reach thirty, the firm was to be sold to a friend of Martin's, Sir Joseph Blake of Tilbury Foundries. The price was even named: ten thousand pounds, and an annuity of eight hundred to the surviving son. By the money values of the time that was giving it away, and judging by today's values – ' He shook his head, as though unable even to try and calculate.

'Yes, but so what, Peter? The clause was fulfilled. Hal was over thirty at the time of his accident, and William lived on for years. What's so important about it now?'

'Everything is important about it, my dear. You see, Hal wasn't thirty at all.' Once again Trew reached in his case and pulled out a little blue-bound book which glinted in the fading light.

'No, Hal was only twenty-nine when he died, and this little devil proves it.'

★ ★ ★

'As soon as I heard that he didn't kill you, old boy, that's when I began to suspect the truth.' The memory of Mott's words was very loud in John's head, almost as though they were in the car together.

'No, he didn't kill you when he had the chance. He pulled aside at the last moment, and that's what told me the story was somehow connected with the Lents. He had no scruples in rubbing out a little, unimportant bookseller, but he couldn't risk hurting Julia.'

John crouched over the wheel of his car, and he'd never driven faster. Mercifully it was Saturday, with the City and East End streets quiet, but at any moment he felt that his luck might run out; a lorry pulling in front of him to force a collision, or a police siren sounding at his back. He pushed the thought away and concentrated on the person he was up against.

For he and Mott had learned a good deal about Peter Trew that morning. A friend of Mott's, the financial editor of a Sunday newspaper, had given them a lot of information, and though neither of them had ever seen the man, his personality was coming into focus. The Trews had worked for the Lent family for generations, and Peter was stamped in the tradition of service. A killer perhaps, but not a monster. Just the loyal servant who would stop at nothing to protect the family's interest.

'Look out!' John's hand came down on the horn, and a short, bespectacled man leapt for his life from a pedestrian crossing. Normally he hated driving fast, but it seemed necessary now – very necessary.

No, Trew wasn't a monster, and he wasn't a lunatic, but he was unbalanced all right; the way Hess and Himmler were unbalanced, probably. He followed a cause, a dream, and he would commit any abomination to serve it. But if the cause let him down, if he woke up out of the dream . . . John accelerated still harder as he thought about that.

All the same, he knew what would happen all right. He was no great judge of women, but he knew how Julia would react. The old man was dead, and she was the last of the line, so Trew had taken her down to the factory to show what he'd saved for her. All his life, all his family's life had been spent in serving the Lents, and he'd killed three times to protect them. He'd tell her what he'd done very proudly, like a dog bringing his mistress a dead rat.

But Julia wouldn't be pleased with Trew's rat, she'd be horrified. And once Trew saw that – once he knew that he'd killed for nothing – once the disciple realized that he was rejected, and the worshipper found that his god was just a clay idol – then adoration might turn into something very different.

'What do you think you're doing?' John braked hard, but it was too late. An enormous, chauffeur-driven Rolls resisted his attempt to cut in at the lights, and the two cars came to rest clutching each other.

'What do I think I'm a'doing, indeed!' The window was rolled down and a red, turkey-cock face under a blue cap glowered out at him.

'It's what you're doing that we want to know about!' He jerked a thumb at the figure of his employer stretched out asleep on the back cushions. It was partly covered by a copy of the *Financial Times*, and the face above the paper looked like a side of uncooked ham.

'Do you know who I'm drivin'? Sir Jasper Grabbin, that's who! If you'd shaken Sir Jasper up, you'd have paid for it all right.' Turkey-cock was clearly starting to enjoy himself.

'Why, for thirty years I've been a chauffeur, and never have I seen a performance like yours. Ought to be ashamed of yerself, you did.'

'My good man, the fact that you've been a menial most of your life is of no interest to me, and I'm in a hurry. Please pull your hearse or butcher's van out of the way, and let me get on.' John watched Turkey's face change from red to scarlet and black, and then the lights changed. He put down his foot and the car shot forward, plucking a side mirror from the Rolls as it did so. For a moment the air was filled with an agonized wailing of horns, and then he was through the traffic and out of earshot.

It was a long drive, and it seemed like eternity, but at last he was there, charging up a side road flanked by office buildings which ended in a pair of gates topped by the enormous black letters A.E.C. He brought the car to a sickening halt with its bonnet almost touching the gates, and then leapt out and rested his hand on a bell at their side.

'All right – all right. Just what is it? I may be hard of hearing, but I'm not deaf, you know.' If the watchman had been dressed in red, he would have made an excellent Father Christmas. He had a neatly trimmed beard, round pink cheeks, and an educated, but rather highly pitched voice.

'Ah, there you are, man. Please let me in at once –' John started to say, but was instantly cut short as Father Christmas squealed with indignation.

'What's that you said? Don't you dare to "man" me, sir. The name is Paget – Mister Paget, and let me tell you something: I may be merely the Night Vigilance Officer here, but before I discovered how much I loathed boys, I was second master at one of the best preparatory schools in the country. Can't say I like adults any better.' As though to drive home the point, he pulled a rubber truncheon from his duffle coat and twirled it menacingly. 'Well, state your business. Just what do you want?'

'Mr Paget.' John fought to make his voice low and humble. 'Have Miss Lent and Mr Trew arrived yet? It's terribly important I see them at once.'

'Oh, that's who you want, is it? Why couldn't you say so at once?' The names of the managing director and the owner of the firm brought no respect to Paget's voice. He seemed to imagine he was a prince of watchmen, as unsackable as an Anglican bishop. Very slowly he brought out a key and started to unlock the wicket gate.

'Yes, they're here all right. You'd better come into my hut and wait for them to come down.'

'No, no, I won't wait, thank you. Just tell me where they are, please. Mr Paget, you must tell me. It's terribly important that I find them.'

'*Must* tell you!' The man almost capered with fury. 'Don't you dare to tell me what I must do, or what's important or not. My job is to keep unauthorized persons from wandering about the site, and that includes you. Besides, you won't find them. They've gone up to the roof of the Tower Block. Only one hoist working there now, and Mr Trew took it. I haven't got a key to any of the doors, and I wouldn't give you one if I had. You'll just have to wait.'

'Oh, no I won't.' John had seen a parked car across the yard, and already he was sprinting towards the great, unfinished building that arched over the factory like a medieval keep of steel and glass. It looked as impregnable as a keep, too, with its huge bronze doors and metal-framed windows, and there was only one weak point in the defences: the cage of the hoist twisting up like a thread against the wall.

But he couldn't climb it. He'd always hated heights, and the very sight of that towering lattice-work made him feel sick and ill. He'd lose his grip before he was a third of the way up.

No, he couldn't climb it. All he could do was to stand there and pray, while at the top a man who had killed three times for an idol might see his idol reject him and kill again. He looked up at the huge expanse above him, and he knew that he had to try to climb it. Even if he broke his neck half way he had to do that. He took off his coat, grasped the first row of girders, and started to pull himself up.

Fifteen

'No, Julia, Hal Lent wasn't thirty when he died. He still had three days to go.' Trew leaned back against the side of the hut, and held out the book to her.

'You see, the accident didn't take place on the sixteenth as William said, but on the thirteenth. Three little days which could have given the firm to Tilbury Foundries.'

'You mean William hid the body?' Julia could only stare at him, and her own body felt as though it were made of ice.

'That's right – he was a real man, was Mr William. By all accounts he and Hal were very close, and the accident must have been a terrible thing for him. All the same, he remembered what was in old Martin's will, and that there were still three days to go before their birthday. If it were known that Hal had died before he was thirty, he would lose control of the firm, and he did the only thing he could. He carried Hal's body down to a cave at the foot of the mountain and packed it with snow. It was snowing hard up there, though it was only October.

'And then he waited. Three whole days he waited beside the body, praying that nobody would find him, that nobody had seen the accident, that Hal wouldn't start to rot. They'd been camping out, of course, so there was no question of their being missed, but it must have been a very horrible three days. Then, on the sixteenth, he put the body back on the scree and went down to the village. Yes, quite a man, was old William Lent.'

'And how did you know all this, Peter?'

'Because I was told, Julia.' There was an odd hint of pride in Trew's voice. 'There have never been any secrets between your family and mine, have there? For fifty years that story has been held by the Lents and the Trews, like a bond binding us together. And now you've heard it, Julia, and the line is complete.'

'Yes, now I've heard it too.' She took the book from him, and glanced at the photograph he had laid open, seeing nothing but rocks, and hills, and the two dots which were climbers.

'But what does this show?'

'It shows the truth – that Hal died on the thirteenth of the month. You see, on that date some crazy Scottish laird was celebrating the death of Butcher Cumberland – the Duke of Cumberland who smashed Bonnie Prince Charlie's rising. He lit a bonfire on the hill here, and had his tenants dance round it. With a magnifying glass you can see it all.

'Yes, this damned photograph tells the whole story, and it could have given the firm to Tilbury Foundries all right. They'd have a hard legal battle, but I think they'd win. "He who comes to Equity must come with clean hands," as the law says, and you couldn't call Bill Lent's hands clean. There was only one thing we could do: get hold of every copy of the book and destroy them.'

'But why now? Why suddenly, after all these years, should it become important?'

'Because a devil found it, Julia. The original photographer happened to read a book on eccentric wills, and came across that clause in old Martin's. Then something must have clicked, and he studied the picture and hit on the truth.' Trew looked away from her and stared down over the factory. His voice was very low and distant.

'I'll never forget how the Chief looked as he opened that letter. He almost seemed to wither as he read it, as though the whole world was collapsing around him. It was a horrible letter, too. That man, Blythe, wasn't just a blackmailer. He wanted to inflict pain as well. I remember how it ended. "All your life has been spent living on stolen money, but now comes the reckoning." Your uncle wanted to try and buy him off, but I knew it was useless. There was only one way to deal with people like the Reverend David Blythe.'

'Then what happened, Peter?' The question was quite meaningless. She knew the truth now.

'Blythe died, Julia. He died three days after he had written that letter, and he talked before he died. We got the whole story, and then we burned his books and his pictures.'

'You mean you killed him?' Julia almost staggered out of the gloom of the hut as Trew smiled at her. His mild, gentle face was more horrible to her than if it had been a grinning devil mask.

'No, no, I didn't kill him, but I arranged for him to die. Hired killers do exist, you know, and I was able to employ the very best. Don't worry about it, though. My man won't talk. He's a professional, with a code of honour like a doctor or lawyer. Besides, he's quite satisfied with our arrangement. At the moment he's on the way to South America, with fifty thousand pounds to his credit at the Bank of Rio de Janeiro. But look out, Julia, there's a gap beside you!' Trew's smile changed to a look of deep concern as she started to stumble away from him.

'Yes, I'll look out, Peter.' Julia stared down over the lip of an air-shaft – a narrow tube of steel and concrete loosely covered by boards. Its walls were lined with pipes and cables, and though more than eight feet square it seemed to taper to nothing before it reached the basement. There was something horribly sinister about that narrowing funnel, but for a moment she almost welcomed the thought of throwing herself over the edge.

'And Roach? You killed him too?'

'Yes, Roach was either greedy or he'd stumbled on the truth. I employed him to buy up copies of the book, and in time he began to ask quite absurd prices. I never knew if he was just a silly old man or was preparing for blackmail, but I couldn't take a chance. I never take chances where the firm is concerned.'

'No, you wouldn't take a chance, Peter.' She moved away from the shaft and stared up at his face. 'And the old clerk at the publishers? I suppose you had him killed as well?'

'Marsden? Yes, that's right. I was rather sorry about him, but my man said it was necessary. We'd have had to kill Cain too, but there's no need now that we have the last copy. We did try and kill him once, but you were there.' Trew lowered his face slightly as he spoke.

'Julia, please believe me. If anything had happened to you from the car that night – if anything had gone wrong – I promise you that I'd have killed myself as well.'

'Yes, I believe you, Peter.' As Julia looked at his face bent towards the floor, she saw that the expression was like a dog's. A loyal, devoted dog that wants nothing except to please its owner. A clever dog that has just retrieved a stick, and expects to be rewarded with a pat.

'And did my uncle know what you'd done?'

'No, not at the beginning, but I told him after Roach died. He was very upset, but I think he knew I was right. Yes, just at the very end he knew I was right. You see, though it might be difficult for Tilbury to prove a claim, we couldn't risk a court case.' He took the book from her as he spoke.

'But there's no need to worry now, Julia. To my certain knowledge this is the last copy, and as soon as I've destroyed the picture we're safe. By the way, I hope you don't mind my calling you Julia. Somehow I feel I've earned the right.'

'I don't mind what you call me.' She looked at his thin, nondescript figure standing against the parapet with the cooling-towers and workshops spread out behind, and she felt no horror or revulsion, but only a terrible sadness. To her the factory was just bricks and steel and concrete, but to him it was the whole world, the meaning of his life. Trew wasn't just a cold-blooded killer, but a company servant fighting to preserve the thing he loved. A monster perhaps, but it was the Lents who inspired that strange, mad loyalty who were really to blame.

'And I don't want you to destroy the book, Peter,' she said very quietly. 'I have a use for it, you see. I'm going to send it to Tilbury Foundries with my compliments.'

'What! To Tilbury!' for a second his face dropped, and then he smiled again.

'Oh, I see, with the plate cut out. Yes, that might be quite amusing.'

'No, no, I'm not joking, Peter. I mean exactly what I say. You see, I never wanted control of the firm. I told you that outside Uncle's bedroom yesterday, but you didn't even listen. Oh, Peter, can't you understand? You've killed for nothing – you've killed three people for nothing!'

'For nothing! No, you're joking of course. You have to be joking. You can't mean what you say.' The Devil's voice could have sounded just like that when Christ rejected all the power of the world.

'But don't make fun of me any more, Julia. Don't laugh at me, little Julia. You're the only one of the family left, so please don't laugh at me. You see, I saved it all for you.' His hands came up on her shoulders, forcing her to look out over the factory, which seemed like a child's model spread out below them. Thin, office-worker's hands, but still strong enough to kill her.

'Yes, it's all yours now, so look at it, Julia. This is where we began; the first little factory that grew up into an empire. Just one of thirteen now, and soon there'll be more – lots more. So tell me you were joking, Julia. Please tell me you were only joking. Oh, my God!' As he stared at her, Trew's face suddenly seemed to wither. Like the rind of an apple peeled away, all expression left it, to show nothing but bewilderment and pain. The face of a wax doll melting before the fire.

'No, no, you're not joking, are you? You're not joking at all.' There was no mistaking the mania in his voice now. 'Why, you're not even a Lent – you can't be a Lent. A Lent would have been pleased with what I'd done – would have thanked me. No, no, you're no Lent. Your mother perhaps – ' His fingers came up to her throat, and he started to laugh, but Julia couldn't even struggle against him. She was just tired – tired of everything – and even as Trew began to kill her, she pitied him.

'Yes, that's it; not a Lent. Just a dirty little cuckoo in the nest, and I've killed three times for you.' The fingers were red-hot metal on her throat now, and there was nothing left in the world except pain, and that choking, mad laughter with the rush of words pouring through it. 'Not a Lent – not a Lent – not a Lent – '

And then suddenly Trew stopped laughing and threw her aside. It wasn't from contempt or disgust that he did that, but because they were no longer alone on the roof. As though in a dream she watched John Cain's hands grip the parapet, and his face rise above it – a face that in a few seconds might be beaten to pulp.

Peter Trew picked up a crowbar which some workman had left lying on the roof, and swung it over his shoulder. There was something almost absurd in the sight of his thin, urban figure wielding a rusty bar of iron, but nothing absurd about his face. For it was the face of the defeated; of one who knows he has lost, but hopes to take a final enemy with him on the long journey. A face which only a cliché could describe; a cornered rat who will get in one slash at the terrier's throat before the jaws hold him. Peter Trew was a monster, but she couldn't hate him – she couldn't even fear him, for it was her family that had made him the terrible thing he was. All the same, she had to stop him.

'Peter,' she said, and her voice sounded quite different. It was filled with all the authority that had built an empire out of three tarred sheds.

'Peter, drop that bar! My name is Lent, Peter, Julia Lent, and I order you to drop it.'

Trew didn't drop the bar, but he hesitated for an instant, and it was enough for John was over the parapet and coming at him. As he did so, Trew stepped to the side, but this time his feet didn't find firm steel and concrete. A board tilted like a see-saw and threw him forward towards the lip of the ventilating shaft. To her dying day Julia would remember the look on his face as he went down.

It took him perhaps ten seconds to reach the ground, and pieces were torn from his body as he fell.

Sixteen

'Yes, I suppose, in a way, we can both claim to have saved each other's life.' Julia grinned at John through the gloom of his shop. It was over a week since they'd last met, and she looked wonderful; almost shining with life and vitality, and quite different from the screaming, sobbing creature he had found on the roof of the building.

'I'm glad I found you in, John. I've got some news for you.'

'Yes, I expected that, but you're too late, I'm afraid. I heard it on the radio a few hours ago. They've caught Palmer.'

'Palmer! Oh, yes, the killer that Peter Trew hired. Yes, he was arrested in Rio this morning. It seems that Peter left a diary giving all the details.' She looked away from John and stared at the shelves.

'Poor Peter,' she said. 'You know, though he tried to kill both of us, though he caused the deaths of three people, I still feel grateful to him in a way. He wanted nothing for himself – just for the Lents – for me.'

'Yes, poor Peter.' John remembered the stuff that had covered the floor of the ventilating shaft. It hadn't looked human at all. It hadn't even looked as though it had once been alive.

'And poor Julia too. I suppose you will be poor now. Tilbury Foundries will take the lot?'

'No, not the lot. They've been very sensible really, and nobody wanted to take the case to court and give the lawyers a field day. They've accepted full control of the firm, and a half-share in the profits. I'll still be a rich woman, it seems. Thanks, John.' She accepted a cigarette from his crumpled packet, and pulled out a little gold lighter.

'And do you know, I'm delighted. There was a time when the thought of being rich terrified me, but not now. I suddenly seem to have woken up and seen things in their right perspective. But, John dear, what's the matter? Aren't you pleased?'

'No, I'm not really pleased.' He bent towards the lighter. It had probably cost more than he made in the average week.

'But what's your other news?'

'Oh, that. I'll tell you in a minute.' There was an odd look of embarrassment in her face, and she glanced at the pile of books he had bought from Mrs Brassey.

'You've been collecting some junk, haven't you?'

'Yes, I'm afraid I have. Should we call it an act of charity? I paid three quid for them.'

'Three pounds! You'll be needing charity yourself, my dear, if you go on like that. *With the Flag to Pretoria*, *Sixty Years a Queen*, *The Poetical Works of Samuel Rogers*. Quite a pretty little binding, but who reads Sam Rogers these days? Let me see, though. There's something rather odd about this one.' She slid her fingers under the covers and bent the book slightly. Like a conjuring trick the gilt edges faded, and a landscape seemed to leap into focus: a bright painting of a farmhouse beside a stream, with a ridge of hills stretching away in the distance. The picture had been painted while the book was twisted in a vice, and only became apparent when held at the same angle.

'Ye Gods!' John bowed his head slightly in admiration. 'No, not charity, but a very nice Victorian fore-edge painting. Not double-edged, I'm afraid, but still worth thirty quid of anybody's money. Thanks, Julia. I never spotted it. You'd make quite a good book-seller.'

'Yes, I think I might, if anybody took me into partnership.' She pushed the book away from him with a slight gesture of irritation.

'But I'd better tell you my news. Jimmy has asked me to marry him.'

'Jimmy? Oh yes, of course, I've heard of him.' An image of the chinless sprig of Scots nobility named Jimmy Stuart-Vale flickered across John's memory. He figured prominently in the glossier magazines as a Debs' Delight, and was just the sort of person that girls like Julia always did seem to marry.

'And have you accepted him?'

'No, I said I wanted a couple of days to think it over. He's rather

a wonderful man, you know. When I told him how neurotic I was
– how I imagined that any man who married me would be after
money – he just laughed and said there was a very simple solution.
I should make over half of everything I owned to him, and never
worry again. Isn't he clever, John?'

'Yes, extremely clever.' John felt slightly sick. In his own mind he
felt Mr Stuart-Vale could best be described as 'a right bastard'.

'And so kind too.' She prattled on like a schoolgirl. 'He says he's
bound to be on the next Honours List, and he's promised to take
the title of Lord Lent. In that way we can keep the firm in the
family name. His own name is much better than ours, of course,
but – '

'But he just wanted to please you.' John's voice was a snarl of
contempt, but Julia seemed past hearing criticism of her precious
Jimmy.

'Yes, that's right, and doesn't it show what a fine man he is?'

'It does indeed. And, if you accept, when will this wedding take
place?'

'Some time next month, at Saint Mark's, Eaton Square. I wanted
to have it very quiet, but Jimmy says he has a debt to his public.

'And the honeymoon afterwards! Oh, he did make that sound
exciting. We'll take my yacht – his yacht it will be then, of course
– to the Bosporus, and then we're going to follow the route of
Alexander the Great's army right through to India.'

'The devil you are!' Once again a picture flitted through John's
head, and he saw the beautiful Julia Lent, beautiful no longer, but
worn and travel-stained as a Bedouin woman, trudging behind a
camel ridden by the Honourable James Stuart-Vale.

No, by heaven he didn't! Stuart-Vale had no part in the picture,
and it was a very different figure who swayed pompously on that
camel's hump.

'Julia,' he said. 'You don't mean – you can't mean – Mott?' He
could hardly bring himself to pronounce the name.

'Yes, of course I do; who else? Jimmy Moldon Mott. Didn't you
know his Christian name was James?'

'No, I didn't know that. I didn't know there was anything Chris-

tian about him. But, Julia, my dear, you can't. You mustn't marry
him. You mustn't even think of it. Why, the man's a monster
and – ' He broke off as he saw the laughter in her face.

'No of course I can't,' she said. 'But there's only one thing that
will stop me.'

'Yes, John,' she started to say. 'If you want to save me from
Mott, you'll just have to – ' She broke off as he came round from
behind the desk, and there was nothing more to be said.